Glas

Ac
The
No
Ph

This bo
renew
date, ₂

0

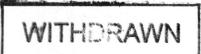

A WOMAN'S TOUCH

Fenn Adams had loved White Waters, her Uncle Simon's farm in Africa, from the very first moment. Before long, however, Fenn realised that not all her uncle's neighbours welcomed her presence. The lovely Helene Starr seemed to particularly resent her — especially when Dr Jason Kemp had agreed to Fenn helping in his bush hospital. Though it seemed that Jason saw Fenn as little more than a child, her feelings for him were those of a woman. And perhaps Jason was in need of a woman's touch . . .

Books by Emma Stirling
Published by The House of Ulverscroft:

EMMA STIRLING

◆

A WOMAN'S TOUCH

Complete and Unabridged

ULVERSCROFT
Leicester

First published in Great Britain in 1996 by
Severn House Publishers Limited, Surrey

Originally published in Great Britain
under the title 'Jacaranda Wedding'
and pseudonym Elspeth Couper

First Large Print Edition
published 1997
by arrangement with
Severn House Publishers Limited, Surrey

British Library CIP Data

Stirling, Emma
    A woman's touch.—Large print ed.—
    Ulverscroft large print series: general fiction
    1. English fiction—20th century
    2. Large type books
    I. Title II. Couper, Elspeth. Jacaranda wedding
    823.9'14 [F]

    ISBN 0-7089-3676-8

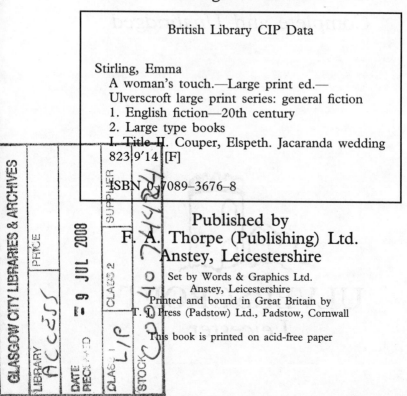

Published by
F. A. Thorpe (Publishing) Ltd.
Anstey, Leicestershire
Set by Words & Graphics Ltd.
Anstey, Leicestershire
Printed and bound in Great Britain by
T. J. Press (Padstow) Ltd., Padstow, Cornwall

This book is printed on acid-free paper

1

FENN ADAMS could not be sure
of the exact moment when she
threw all caution to the winds in
deciding to accept her uncle's invitation
to spend six months with him on his farm
in Africa. Returning from a frustrating
day at the office where she worked as
secretary to old Mr Hoy, kind and
understanding as he was, Uncle Simon's
letter had been waiting.

It painted such an enchanting picture
of the blue skies and bright sunshine of
Africa, and having just emerged from
the hurrying crowds on the buses and
subways of London's rush hour, the
perpetual rain that, this winter seemed
never ending, the letter seemed to Fenn
the embodiment of all her dreams. She
had let herself into the dimly lit hallway of
the tall Victorian house where she rented
a small apartment, and immediately her
eyes were drawn to the long white
envelope propped on the hall table.

The blue and white airmail edging; the colourful stamps depicting some exotic bird told her it was from her uncle. But before she could lift it in one slim hand Mrs Evans, her landlady, extremely curious about Uncle Simon's life in a 'far off land', appeared and called, "A letter from your uncle, Miss Adams! Always brings a bit of sunshine into my life, does his letters."

Fenn smiled and ran upstairs to read in the peace of her room. The letter had 'White Waters, Umzunpilo', in the top right hand corner.

After the usual greetings he wrote, "Since the death of your aunt last year I have been lonely, but I did not realize how lonely until I received your card on the occasion of my birthday. Sixty-five! How time flies! I must say it was a card I treasured. You always were a sweet child, Fenn, and it would seem as if you have grown into an equally sweet and understanding woman. How old are you now? Twenty? Twenty-one? And no attachments from what I gather! So, if you have no objection, I would very much like you to come out to Africa and make your home here with me at White Waters. Try it for a period of, say, six months. I guarantee you will love it. As I write the jacaranda are in full bloom, lining the driveway that leads to my house. Long, drooping tassels of mauve that from where I sit look as though they cover the trees in a lilac veil . . ."

He ended with a dejected little sentence, "Like me, however, White Waters needs a woman's touch . . . "

There was more, of course. Details of flights, of money arrangements. Why not, she thought? Why not visit her uncle for an extended holiday? At twenty she longed for something more than shiny wet city pavements and traffic-jammed streets.

By the weekend Fenn's decision was made. She gave her notice to Mr Hoy, explaining the reason, and was touched to see the startled expression that appeared on his face. "Central Africa!" he breathed. "But — but isn't that rather — ahem — dangerous, Miss Adams? And alone, and you such a young girl." He pronounced it 'gel'.

"I shall be going to live on my uncle's

farm, Mr. Hoy," Fenn reminded him. "It has the most unusual name, White Waters, and is set in a valley where they grow maize, and my uncle also has some horses and cattle." She smiled. "You see, I won't be completely alone or in the wilderness."

Mr Hoy's faded eyes looked at her fondly. He had grown to appreciate this young girl with the dark hair and blue eyes who was quiet and respectful, not at all like some of the other young ladies in the office . . . He knew something of Fenn's history, of the tragic death of her parents, two years ago.

Fenn dreamed that night of the glorious summer when she had been ten and she and her uncle had gone riding across the sands at daybreak. Her mother had been so excited to see her large, good-natured brother from across the seas and Fenn straight from the start had fallen under the spell of his genial charm. Now she would see him again. She could hardly believe that in so short a time she would be leaving behind the familiar everyday scenes of her old life; Big Ben standing against a red and gold sunset; red double-decker buses pouring along Oxford Street, their passengers vanishing into the huge stores . . .

Now she was heading for a continent steeped in history, a land of veldt and forests and blue jacaranda trees . . . She dozed intermittedly during the flight and woke to the sunshine and blue skies of Africa, and saw for herself the jacaranda in full bloom. At the Airport she went through customs, returning the welcoming smiles of the African Airport officials. The sun was blinding. After the winter chill of London in November, however, it seemed wonderful on her bare head and shoulders. What would her uncle look like? Ten years was a long time. Had the death of his dearly loved wife changed him all that much?

Now when she saw the tall man coming towards her she wondered for a moment, then saw he was much too young to be her uncle. This man would be in his early thirties.

"Miss Adams?" he queried, "Miss Fenn Adams?" At Fenn's nod of assent he continued. "I was sent by your uncle to meet you."

His rather shy smile made him look much younger, his blue eyes crinkling at the corners in the manner of a man who spends much of his time outdoors, gazing across sunfilled spaces. He collected her suitcases and walked with her across the tarmac, soft in the heat of the sun, to where a car, a dusty station wagon, stood under the shade of some trees. A porter followed with the rest of Fenn's luggage which he stowed in the back.

"I'm Frank Telfer," the young man went on to explain. "Your uncle employs me to help with the business side of the farm. Your uncle wasn't able to make the trip. His heart troubles him sometimes and he has to take it easy."

"I had no idea," Fenn said. "I'm sorry to hear that. Maybe I'll be too much trouble . . . "

"Oh, he's all right," Frank assured her quickly. "It's just that his doctor advised him not to overdo it and this journey into town is one of the things he prefers not to undertake." He grinned at her puzzled expression. "The heat, you know, combined with our so-called roads." His grin widened. "You'll see," he promised.

They were soon driving along a road flanked by flamboyant trees in full flower. Occasionally there was a group of jacarandas, their blue blossom contrasting delicately against the bright red of the flamboyants. The road slowly climbed until the view all round was breathtaking. Fenn looked out over a sun-freckled valley where apricot-smudged tracks divided the terraced hills and an occasional red-roofed farmhouse, half concealed in thick clumps of shade trees, stood in isolated splendour.

Frank at last turned into a long tree-lined driveway, the driveway of her uncle's description, at the end of which a long white single-storied house came into view.

"White Waters," Frank murmured, smiling down at Fenn's surprised face. She had been prepared for a tin-roofed brick house, or even a thatched one.

"It's very lovely," she breathed. Frank looked pleased. "Your uncle thinks there's no place like it in the country.

It's very comfortable and as he has extremely efficient house servants, as well as gardeners, quite an achievement in this country, the running of it is no trouble." He paused for a moment, looking down at her. "After your aunt died last year he thought for a while of selling up and going back to England. But after years in this climate he realized how foolish it would be. Besides, White Waters is his life now.

He smiled apologetically. "But here I am, detaining you in this heat while you must be dying to see your uncle."

As they alighted from the car at the foot of the verandah steps, Frank calling to an African servant nearby to take Fenn's luggage into the house, Simon Chase appeared, followed by a large dog, its silky red coat gleaming in the bright sunshine.

"My dear Fenn, how lovely to see you," her uncle greeted her. He took her by the shoulders and kissed her on one cheek. Then, standing back a little but still holding her shoulders, he exclaimed, "But how grown-up you've got! Quite the young lady."

Fenn smiled. "Ten years is a long time, uncle." A shadow crossed his face. "Yes, indeed it is." She could see he was thinking not only of his own loss but also of her own when both her parents had died so suddenly two years ago . . .

He was a tall man, with thick silvery hair and the red weather-beaten complexion from being much in the open air. Fenn, whose mother had been his 'little sister', and his favourite, had the same firm chin, but where the blue of Simon Chase's eyes had faded with age Fenn's was the blue of a mountain lake with the sun on it; eyes that gazed placidly at the world from a small oval face under a cloud of dark hair. There was none of the shy gaucheness that her uncle remembered from ten years ago.

"Let me show Miss Adams to her room, Simon," Frank said. "Then we can all sit and talk."

After a bath fragrant with exotic bath salts, Fenn dressed herself in a simple cotton dress of lime green trimmed with white, brushed her dark hair until it shone, added a touch of bright lipstick and thrust her bare feet into white

9

sandals. It was too hot for pantihose.

She found her uncle and Frank already seated on the comfortable-looking cane chairs on the verandah and came forward hesitantly, feeling suddenly shy with these two strange men. For, even though Simon Chase *was* her uncle, the ten years between ten and twenty seemed like an eternity to Fenn now.

The red setter, Sean, lay at their feet, eyes half closed but missing nothing. At her appearance Frank jumped to his feet, pulling out a chair while her uncle called, "Come on, my dear, have some tea. Bet you feel like it, eh, after that drive? These days I make it as little as possible, don't I Frank?"

"How long have you been with my uncle, Frank?" Fenn queried with interest. The two men exchanged glances. "Oh, about eight years, isn't it, Simon? You had bought the farm two years previously and it wasn't doing so well, remember?"

Simon smiled, remembering. "And within months of our joining forces White Waters was prospering," he answered.

Frank nodded and Fenn, curious,

asked, "Tell me, why do you call it 'White Waters'? It's a lovely name but I don't recall seeing any rivers or lakes as we drove up."

"The Africans hereabouts have quite an unpronounceable name for it, which, as near as we will ever get, translated, means just that, where-the-waters-are-white. Maybe ages ago there was a great lake here, or a river, and the name had lingered. We liked it and decided to retain it."

Her uncle smiled. "When Frank first came here, he was straight out of Agricultural school and being young had a romantic notion that, like a ship, one should never change the name of a farm or a house; brings bad luck and all that nonsense."

"And you didn't change it and you've had *good* luck," Fenn exclaimed. "What a lovely sentiment!"

"Now," she went on, putting on an energetic tone. "Let's first finish our tea then Frank can show me about the farm, if," gazing at the solemn young man a little shyly, "if you aren't too busy, Frank? I realize the work of a place this size never stops and far be it for me to interrupt your normal daily routine. In fact, act just as though I weren't here."

Frank's lips twisted into a slight smile. He gazed down at the small upturned face, the blue eyes smiling at him with such friendship, the dark hair lying shiningly on the shoulders of the green dress, then transferred his gaze to Simon Chase. "Don't you think, sir, that might be a little difficult? To act as though your niece were not here? As far as I can see, she is going to cause quite a bit of havoc in the valley."

Fenn's eyes opened wide. "Why? Why should I cause a havoc in the valley?"

Simon stood up, smiling, brushing the cake crumbs from the front of his cream coloured safari jacket. "Frank's teasing you, child. Take no notice of him. Come, I'll show you over the house and Frank can take you over the grounds tomorrow."

2

A FEW days later Fenn stood gazing through the windows of the breakfast room. The rain of the night had cleared and the view was a revelation. Sunshine; a sky, so vivid a blue it hurt one's eyes to gaze at it, while below the window one of the gardeners was cutting the lawn, voice deep in his throat as he sang in rhythm to the rise and fall of his 'panga', a broad-bladed knife much in use in this part of Africa. Through the open window the smell of wet earth and freshly cut grass was exhilarating. The rain during the night had been so sudden as to be frightening. The thunder of it on the farmhouse roof had wakened her and hurriedly snatching the gown that lay at the end of her bed, she had stood by the window, watching the parched earth as it soaked greedily at the rain. The pointsetta bush just outside her window bowed its crimson head under the onslaught.

Then, as suddenly as it began it stopped and a deep silence followed, broken only by the rhythmical plop-plop of the rain pipes. Birds appeared, for the day was not far from the horizon, and Fenn's spirits soared with the birds.

There was all the promise of another hot day. After the grey, wet winter which she had just experienced she felt she would never get enough of this hot, bright sunshine.

She turned from the window as her uncle came into the room, carrying the morning paper that was specially delivered to the railway siding three miles away and collected each morning by a picanin on a bicycle.

"Humph, up already, my dear?" he said as she went to meet him. "Hope the rainstorm did not frighten you. It takes quite a bit of getting used to. Now what do you propose to do today?"

"I thought I'd ride out and see some of the farm," Fenn told him. "If I wouldn't be in anyone's way." She bit appreciatively into the slice of paw-paw sprinkled with lemon juice. She thought this ideal for breakfast, its cool, sweet taste mingling with the bite of the lemon juice was the very thing to greet a hot, sun-filled day. There was a boiled egg and slices of home-made bread, the most delicious she had ever tasted.

The marmalade and jams were all home-made, too, and she had said on her first day to Daisy, hovering attentively around, "This is very good! Who makes them?"

"Ellias — Cook," was the answer and Fenn later discovered Ellias had been her uncle's cook for a very long time, being trained by Uncle Simon's wife when she first came to the farm. Ellias also made the most wonderful sponge cake that melted in the mouth and his tasty snacks for 'sundowners' would have satisfied the most fastidious London hostess.

Now her uncle said, "By all means go round the farm if you would like to. But take my warning and wear a big hat. Frank has to go down to the siding to see if there's any sign of that new farm machinery. Why don't you go with him? I'm sure he'll be only too glad of your company."

To Frank she had taken a great liking.

He was shy with her, and, she suspected, with most women, and did not say much, but she liked his direct gaze and the old-world gallantry he always showed her. He had taken her round the farm buildings on that first afternoon; shown her the small office with the filing cabinets, desk and typewriter, explaining, "A lot of the farm work is done here, the more tedious work, I'm afraid." And Fenn had murmured that she would be glad to help at any time at which he'd looked horrified and replied, "My goodness, no, Fenn. I wouldn't dream of imposing . . . "

She had followed him through the large cool kitchen, with its red polished floor, deep sinks and huge deep freeze. "A necessity in this country," Frank had explained, seeing her looking at it, thinking how big it was for two people, three now with Fenn. They went out onto the gauze-enclosed verandah where a house servant, spotless in white, was busy ironing, humming to himself all the while, as most of these people seemed to do whilst working. Down the shallow flight of steps she followed, across the glaringly sunfilled dusty compound to a group of white buildings from which music was playing, the throbbing, sometimes mournful music peculiar to Africa.

"Transistor radios," Frank smiled down at her. "Most of the natives own one now. At one time it was a guitar, everyone carried them, now its a transistor."

The walk around was quick, for she suspected Frank was a busy man, with little time for foolish questions from a young girl straight from England. Fenn tried to look intelligent as he talked but most of the time she was completely lost. The African women sitting in the sun outside their homes fascinated her, especially the ones who were doing each other's hair, plaiting the black crinkly strands into tiny plaits, showing the pinkish dark parting beneath.

Numerous children stood about, fingers in mouths, eyes huge as they gazed at this stranger to their Bwana's farm. The lovely red setter, Sean, ran ahead, advancing playful darts at the picanins, making them squeal and clutch at their mother's skirts. Frank eventually called it to heel and it returned, tongue lolling, looking slightly sheepish, as though to assure them it was only playing.

As they walked back to the house Frank had looked down at the slim dark girl by his side. "Well, and how do you think you'll like it, Fenn? You don't mind if I call you that, do you?"

"Of course not, go ahead." She had lifted her face to the sun, feeling its golden kiss on her skin. "I think I shall love it," she went on, in answer to his question.

She saw the amused look on his face as he asked, "You don't think you'll be lonely here? There aren't many neighbours and the few that there are live miles away."

"No, I don't think I'll be bored one little bit. In fact, I'm *sure* I shall love it."

"There's always the Pendletons to visit, Angie is a bit young and foolish, but quite a nice sort, really, if you take into account her age. And you can always go riding together."

"How old is Angie?" Fenn enquired curiously. It would be nice to have another girl about her age in which to confide.

Frank shrugged. "About 18 or 19. They grow up so quickly I'm not absolutely certain. And then of course there's always Miss Starr, Helene Starr, over at Makcome Farm. She's probably more your age, and sensible with it, although she doesn't live here much, spends most of her time abroad or in Cape Town. She's here on a visit to her grandfather who owns Makcome Farm. You'll soon get to meet her, Fenn."

Fenn got the impression that meeting Helene Starr was to be quite an honour . . .

Now bestowing a hasty kiss on the top of her uncle's white head she answered to his suggestion that she go with Frank to the railway siding, "I'd love to go. See you at lunch . . . "

The expedition was enjoyable. Frank was affable, humorous, and informative. He knew the lands belonging to her uncle so well, as well as he knew the country, and she could tell he loved both with a firm and resolute love. He knew the country's wild life, its history, its inhabitants.

They drove first to the river, following

a rough track across the veldt that brought them to the river bank and a bridge spanning the river six or eight miles from the farmhouse. The air was like wine, heady, fragrant with wet grass and even the swaying of the landrover could not spoil the morning for Fenn. She felt like throwing her arms wide and singing. Her eyes twinkled. She wondered what Frank would do if she did. He was so — so prosaic. Probably be shocked to bits, she thought.

"It's such a lovely, lovely morning," she exclaimed. "Is it always like this, Frank?"

Removing his eyes from the bridge over which they travelled, for a brief moment, he smiled down at her. "It very often is. But once the rains set in properly it can be pretty awful. Sometimes the river floods and we're marooned for days at a time. Everything you touch feels damp, and your shoes, unless you wear them turn about, go green and mildewy."

The landrover gave a sudden jolt, throwing her sideways against him.

"Sorry, Fenn," he said, battling with the gears. "The night's rain didn't do

20

this road any good, I'm afraid."

She had to smile at his use of the word, road. They passed African women, huge loads on their heads, pausing as they drove by to gaze after them and discuss animatedly where they might be going, those two white people in the landrover. They knew Frank, but Fenn soon found she was the topic of discussion all over the farm. She could feel a trickle of perspiration on her top lip and between her shoulder blades and thought of the tan she would soon acquire.

How lovely! And in October, too!

They came to a twin track of railway lines shining silver in the sun and while Frank sorted out the boxes and parcels addressed to White Waters, Fenn gazed around her until Frank had finished — then he said: "Well, that seems to be all for White Waters. I see Jason Kemp's got some stuff here. I hope he collects it before the next rainstorm. The siding shed isn't exactly waterproof and old Jason's finding it hard enough going without loosing any of his precious medical supplies."

He helped Fenn into the landrover and

climbed in beside her. Fenn retied the silk scarf around her head ready for the journey back. "Who is Jason Kemp? I don't think I've met him yet."

Frank engaged gear and they ground out of the siding, the African children running behind them, waving and calling shrilly, "'Bye Bwana, bye Donna'."

To their delight Fenn returned their waves then turned back to Frank as he said, "Jason, — or rather, Doctor Kemp, runs a small hospital over by Mluba Hill, roughly about six miles from here. I'm not surprised you haven't met him. He's not exactly the social type, in fact I would say he's definitely anti-social. Doesn't mix much, seldom leaves his hospital."

Fenn sat for a moment, thinking of Doctor Kemp, of the lonely life he must lead, and murmured, "Poor old thing! I suppose he must think its worth it, sacrificing something, to be able to devote his life to the things he thinks are worthwhile."

Frank gave her an amused glance, then said, wryly, "Yes, I suppose you are right."

As they retraced their way back to the farmhouse with its wine red and purple bougainvillaea clinging to the white walls, Fenn thought it was probably the most beautiful home she had ever seen. It looked so peaceful, with Uncle Simon's red setter playing in the driveway, it was hard to believe that Africa, untamed, wild, was waiting with prodigious patience to reclaim the land back . . .

Uncle Simon joined them for lunch. Afterwards Daisy a plump African girl, came back to clear the table and carry a tray of coffee to the verandah where Uncle Simon preferred to spend the afternoon, stretched out in a long cane chair, dozing, his legs in a patch of sunlight. It was very hot. The valley seemed to hover in a heat haze. Fenn sat next to him in a cane chair while Frank hastily drank his coffee then excused himself and vanished into the office. It was so peaceful. Already she loved the quiet serenity of the farm, the perfume of the tropical bushes that dotted the stretch of green lawn, still damp from the night's rain; the loyal companionship of Sean, lying at her uncle's feet, eyes half closed, lazily watching a long green lizard scuttle across the red polished verandah floor and vanish behind a white pot that held scarlet geraniums. Presently Uncle Simon roused himself and said, "Why don't you get one of the boys to saddle Esmeralda and get out while the weather's still fine? The sun has lost some of its heat by now and soon you'll get a cool breeze coming from the hills."

Fenn complied with his bidding and went once more to her bedroom to change. She felt she could not sit still and that it might take quite a time for her to adjust to the leisurely way of life that seemed to be the thing out here. The jodpurs that she had bought in London fitted her slim figure perfectly and in a yellow, open-necked shirt of the finest silk, with a paisley-patterned scarf at the neck, she looked very attractive. As she approached the stable, Sean, the red setter, came ambling forward, sensing an outing. Already he adored Fenn, a fact that made Simon exclaim that she should be honoured. Sean gave his loyalty and affection to very few; her uncle and

Frank Telfer being the only two people the beautiful dog ever welcomed.

He welcomed her now, plume of a tail waving in delighted anticipation of the coming outing, velvet brown eyes gazing up at her hopefully. Fenn laughed aloud. "Oh, all right, pest! Give you an appetite for your dinner."

As she rode out on the nut-brown filly that her uncle had chosen as the most gentle and reliable of his small stable, she blessed the riding lessons her mother insisted she take when she was a teenager, saying she never knew when they might come in handy. After the death of her parents there had been no more money for riding lessons. But the skill had stayed with her and as she cantered across the rough grassland she felt exhilarated.

The sun was still pleasantly warm on her back and shoulders and the night's rain seemed to have released dozens of different flower smells. Here and there the gleam of water reflected the deep blue of the sky. A sudden splash of colour indicated where a clump of veldt flowers grew precariously between a scattering of grey rocks, their faces turned as one towards the sun.

She turned the horse's head towards the gentle rise of green, crossing a shallow river bed where the water came barely up to Esmeralda's hocks. Sean ranged before them, splashing through the water with evident delight. She rode for an hour, the air warm against her face, her hair loose and tangled on her shoulders. Suddenly the landscape seemed familiar. Without noticing she must have ridden towards the railway siding.

The place seemed deserted now and she wondered if many trains came this way. The twin silver lines stretched into the distance, vanishing into a wavy haze of heat. The picanins, squatting in the shade of the huts, were silent.

Suddenly, breaking the stillness, came a noise, a shrill, high cry that to Fenn sounded like a woman in pain, and startled Esmeralda so that she skittered sideways on the path, ears laid back nervously.

Fenn laid a gentling hand on the quivering neck. "There, girl, there!"

The door of one of the huts that lined

the siding opened and a woman emerged. She was old and bent and dressed in black. Red-veined eyes looked up at Fenn from a wrinkled black face. Two yellow teeth appeared as she grinned, seeing Fenn. Before the startled girl could say a word the old woman scurried froward and caught at her stirrup.

"Oh, madam, madam," she cried. "Please help . . . It is my daughter. The baby won't come . . . "

Unable to ignore the piteous look in the old woman's eyes but inwardly quailing, for what did she know about babies? Fenn slipped from her horse and followed the woman into the hut, bending her head as she did so, for the doorway was very low, even for Fenn's five foot four. Inside the darkness was almost total. The air smelled of smoke and it was terrifically hot. In one there appeared to Fenn to be a bundle of rags. On closer inspection, however, she made out a dark face, twisted with pain, and a figure distorted by pregnancy. The girl looked very young and pathetic, lying there on the hard-packed floor, not even a pillow to support her. Fenn needed no experience to know that the girl was in a bad way . . .

"She must get to hospital, — *hospital*," she told the old crone, emphasizing the last word. The woman nodded eagerly. "Yes, hospital — over by Mluba Hill."

"How can we get her there? We must not waste any time."

"Truck . . . Yusaf has truck."

Yusaf turned out to be the railway employee who obligingly offered to drive them. They made the girl as comfortable as they could in the back and Fenn rode with Yusaf in the front, having been assured by the picanins that her horse would be well looked after until her return. The old woman stayed with the girl, crooning over her in a disconsolant way. Twenty minutes later they reached the hill that gave its name to the cluster of buildings that was the hospital.

There was a half dozen white, tin-roofed buildings sparsely draped with golden shower creepers, hugged by a hibiscus hedge ablaze with vivid scarlet blossoms. Over all shimmered a heat haze and the glare in the clearing was dazzling. All the well-trodden footpaths were edged with white-washed stones. Red, yellow and orange canna lilies marched along the paths leading to small open-sided shelters where the out-patients waited their turn for treatment.

As they drew up in the clearing three large dogs rushed excitedly up to them, barking and leaping about the truck. Sean, coward that he was, took one look at them and opted to stay in the truck, pressing against Fenn's knees.

She grinned, patting his head, "I don't blame you. They don't look particularly friendly to me, either."

Yusaf halted the truck in front of the wide verandah and Fenn climbed out, standing uncertainly on the rough grass while the old woman, aided by Yusaf, explained to the African nurse who appeared to know exactly what the trouble was. As they disappeared into a building away from the main house, the sagging body of the young girl between them, the gauze screen door of the verandah opened and a man came down the steps.

"Good afternoon!" His greeting was without warmth. "Sorry if my dogs were being a nuisance." He seemed preoccupied and turned to go indoors again and the dogs, taking no further notice of Fenn or the cowering Sean, followed him up the shallow flight of steps, pushing and shoving to be the one nearest to him.

"Can you tell me where Doctor Kemp is?" Fenn called. "We've just brought a patient . . . "

He turned towards her again. "Hmmm . . . And where is your patient?"

"She was taken to that building, down there," replied Fenn, nodding towards the white block where the girl had disappeared. "I think Doctor Kemp should see her, she's in a bad way. A baby . . . "

His mouth twitched at the corners and he gave her a measured glance that made her feel about ten years old. "My dear child," he went on, adding insult to injury, "these women are used to having their babies in fields and returning ten minutes later to whatever task they were doing before the interruption. I have no doubt she's in good hands."

Fenn was outraged. "I think that is

one of the most heartless remarks I've ever heard."

His mouth twitched again. "Do I know you?" he asked, quite illogically it seemed to Fenn.

"No," she retorted, adding, under her breath, "And I don't particularly want to know *you*, either."

He gave her another look, something in his eyes she could not quite put a finger on, then said, "I know, you're old Simon Chase's niece. I heard about you. How are you enjoying Africa? Not quite the same as the movies and television programmes at home would have it, eh?"

"Oh, I don't know. I've met some very interesting and charming people. Though not all of them were likeable." The innuendo in her words was not lost on him.

His grin widened. "We've plenty of all sorts, here in the valley. But I must go. Pressure of work. Good day."

His curt dismissal staggered her. Used to being noticed by men since she was at high school, she almost felt as if she'd been slapped in the face, hard. She

31

murmured a cool, "Good afternoon," and climbed back into the truck to wait for Yusaf. Sean flopped all over her, clearly delighted that she had rejoined him. A most surly young man, she thought, and one she most fervently hoped was not a friend of her uncle's. He would be one person she would not look forward to meeting a second time. Several angry retorts had jostled in her mind but she had been too angry to voice them. She wondered who he might be and the position he held with Doctor Kemp. If he was as rude to the old doctor as he had been to her — well!

3

THAT evening as she showered and dressed — several showers a day were needed in this hot climate, she had found, — she wondered if she should tell her uncle about the encounter with the girl, but finally decided to say nothing. She did not want her uncle to think she was becoming too involved with the Africans and there was no point in worrying him about something so obviously out of his jurisdiction.

From her selection of dresses she took out a thin silk gown of vibrant burnt orange with tiny pearl buttons held by loops down the front of the bodice. It did wonderful things to her dark hair and creamy skin, just beginning to glow with a golden tan owing to the bright sunshine and the amount of time she spent out of doors. She put on sheer pantihose, the sheerist she possessed, and gold sandals with narrow straps and absurdly high heels.

She returned to her dressing table and began brushing her dark hair until it shone. The door opened and Selina, the African maid, came silently in on bare feet and began to turn down the bed, letting the mosquito net fall in soft white folds about it.

Fenn caught the girl's eye in the mirror and smiled. How strange, not to say pleasant, to have a maid of one's own, to wash and iron for you and tidy away your clothes. Not that Fenn had ever been untidy. Quite the reverse. Selina came near, bending to pick up a pair of dusty shoes Fenn had just discarded.

"I'll clean them, Selina," she told her.

The maid looked horrified, brown eyes widening in the dark face. "They will be cleaned in the kitchen, madam," she said, primly, gazing almost reproachfully at Fenn for suggesting such a thing.

Fenn shrugged and as the maid left the room, gave one last look at her reflection in the mirror.

"Fenn!" It was her uncle's voice calling from the hall. "Our guests are here!"

"Coming, Uncle Simon."

Major and Mrs Pendleton and their daughter Angelina — "Call me Angie, everyone else does," — were seated in the lounge, sampling the delicious sundowners prepared by Frank, who stood quietly in the background, glass in hand, smiling reassuringly at Fenn as she entered. Major Pendleton, retired, as he was at pains to point out, was a tall man with a beaked nose and a red face who laughed a lot and told endless stories of his earlier days in the Colony.

His wife was blonde. Delicate and rather pale she eyed her husband like a fond mother eyeing a too-noisy child, exasperatingly whenever his laughter became too loud. Angie Pendleton was fair, like her mother, — but fair with hair the colour of newly-ripened wheat. She had warm brown eyes and freckles. The skin on her nose was peeling where she had recently caught the sun and a slim brown hand lifted self-consciously every so often to touch it.

Frank did not help and Fenn felt sorry for the girl when he said, more jovially than Fenn had ever seen him,

"Swimming too long in the sun again, Angie? You'll never learn, will you?"

Mrs Pendleton simpered. "Angie's like me, too fair for this wretched climate. We have such delicate skins."

The other guests consisted of a young man, introduced to Fenn as Bill Paynter, and a girl, maybe a little older than herself, as Helene Starr.

Helene was tall, very dark, with glossy hair drawn back into a loose chignon. Her eyes were enormous, like brown pansies, with thick lashes that curled upwards. Her mouth was full and soft, a little sulky, and lightly touched with pale coral lipstick. It was plain that she had little time for her own sex, concentrating her charms on the men of the party. She was very emphatic and talked with an assurance that Fenn envied.

She wore a tight green satin skirt, split up one side, a gold lame blouse with a deep neckline edged with tiny gold coins. Exotic and gypsyish, Fenn thought, but, on Helen, definitely becoming. Against her Fenn felt very ordinary and commonplace. She caught Angie's eye and the girl had the same feeling.

Something seemed to pass between them, a sort of comradeship, an affinity against all the glamorous women of the world.

Bill Paynter was a fair young man with an attractive voice and smiling hazel eyes, which rested frequently on Fenn, making her feel that at least he did not consider Helene the only woman in the room.

"Helene is on one of her periodical visits to her grandfather," Uncle Simon explained as he introduced the two girls. "What a pity she doesn't decide to stay. Always introduces a little glamour into our dull lives, does Helene."

Helene looked at Fenn briefly, smiled, nodded and turned her beautiful dark eyes back to Frank. Soon Fenn found herself sitting on the couch next to Mrs Pendleton and answering questions, sipping the fruit drink Frank had given her with the words, "Fruit juice for you, young lady. Your uncle's instructions, until you get used to our habit of sundowners."

Before long Bill came to sit on her other side. "How do you like it here, Miss Adams? Bit rough after London, eh?"

"Not really. I'm enjoying myself immensely."

Bill pulled a face, making her smile. "Town's got a bit of life. Not much. I'm at University, on vacation just now, otherwise I doubt if I could stand it. You must let me take you sightseeing."

"I'd love that," Fenn answered. "How far away do you live?"

"About eight miles, which practically makes us neighbours. You must ride over sometime and visit us."

Fenn assured him she would be delighted. The conversation turned to other matters. After dinner Fenn led Mrs Pendleton and the two girls back to the lounge where coffee was laid out and the large windows open to the night. A wind had sprung up, bringing with it the heady scent of gardenias, and the air was much cooler.

Fenn poured coffee into the tiny exquisite cups with their blue and gold design and the hovering Daisy handed them around. Angie turned to Fenn, saying, "So you really like it here, do you?"

"It's wonderful. I don't know how

anyone could ever bear to leave it."

Helene, hearing her, laughed sourly and said, "Wonderful! It's deadly! I can hardly wait to get back to civilization once more after a few weeks of this."

Mrs Pendleton frowned at her. "Really, Helene! You'll be giving Fenn a completely erroneous impression. Actually, dear," turning to smile at Fenn, "We do have some very gay times here. The annual native dances will be taking place shortly. You'll have to persuade your uncle to bring you and you can stay overnight with us. Angie will be only too glad of the company. I know how you young girls love to giggle over pop stars and such things."

Angie caught Fenn's eye and made a little face, her mouth turning down at the corners and Fenn had to smile. "I'll look forward to it," she told them. "Providing, of course, my uncle can take the time off. I know how busy the farm keeps him."

Major Pendleton, who by now had joined them with the other men, thrust his hands into his pockets and rocked on his heels, frowning. "Yes, of course it isn't like farming in the old country.

Can't take your eyes off these blighters for a minute without them getting drunk or something."

"Oh, I daresay I can take the odd day off," Uncle Simon smiled. "If anything crops up that prevents it, there's always Frank here. Obliging sort of fellow and I believe he's taken quite a liking to young Fenn."

Fenn laughed, feeling herself flush, and turned towards Angie. She was surprised at the look on the girl's face. A look that combined shock, an involuntary tightening of the mouth and — and something in the brown eyes that had Fenn wondering . . .

"Native dances!" Helene spoke again and there was deep scorn in her voice. "What on earth makes you think Fenn would be interested in them? When one thinks of Sadlers Wells and Covent Garden, all those wonderful first nights, the lovely gowns and jewellery . . . " She sighed, then went on. "And you come to a place like this!"

Fenn found herself answering, almost angrily, "I think White Waters is a wonderful place. I wouldn't have missed this chance for the world."

"I think Fenn's right." Angie spoke now, brown eyes flashing. "I think its a wonderful opportunity for her. I — I only wish *I* had the same chance to travel . . ."

"Now why on earth would a little girl like you want to travel?" Frank spoke and his voice was faintly mocking. "You wouldn't know what to do with yourself away from the farm."

Helene, as though to change the conversation, said, looking at Simon, "Didn't you say you'd invited the recluse?"

Simon nodded. "I did invite him but you know what he is. He said he couldn't make it for dinner but would try and get here for drinks afterwards."

Mrs Pendleton remarked, simperingly, "If he knows Helene is here he'll come."

Everyone smiled at Helene and Fenn watched the colour come up under the other girl's golden tan and thought, "Whoever the recluse is, she's keen on him."

Uncle Simon was speaking. "You know how he feels about that hospital of his.

Won't leave it for a minute."

"I once asked him to a New Year's Eve party I was giving," Mrs Pendleton interjected. "And do you know what he said? That he had not come all the way to Africa to attend parties, and I said, but a New Year's Eve party, doctor, and he said, in that cool, aloof way of his, 'Not even New Year's Eve parties, ma'am'."

"I think I hear him now." Simon was rising and walked to the open french doors. Fenn wondered who they could be talking about and watched as the car headlights curved round the drive and across the lawn and pulled up in front of the verandah. Her uncle went out and came back a moment later, accompanied by Fenn's acquaintance of the afternoon.

"Come on in, Jason," her uncle was saying. "You know Major P and his missus, and of course Angie. And there's Helene and Bill and Frank and . . . "

He turned to Fenn. "And this, Jason, is my niece. Fenn has deserted the bright lights of London to come and live with us for a time at White Waters. Fenn," turning to the dismayed girl and smiling,

42

"I want you to meet Doctor Kemp, who happens to be one of the best things that ever happened to our little community." This last remark was with a grin, affectionate and endearing.

To her consternation Fenn felt herself blushing. Doctor Kemp, the recluse! Whatever must he think of her? And yet, he had been as much to blame.

The tall young doctor gave her a formal bow. "This is most interesting," amusement shining in his grey eyes. "Helene has always considered herself the prettiest girl in our valley, followed closely by Angie of course. Now I can see they will have to look to their laurels."

"I'm sure Miss Adams has heard all this many times before, Jason," Helene murmured, patting the wide settee on which she sat. "Come and sit by me, darling, and tell me what has happened since I saw you last."

Major Pendleton said gruffly, "We were just talking about you, old boy . . . " only to be interrupted by a warning glance from his wife, who went on in the sudden silence, "And how is everything at the hospital, *dear* Doctor Kemp?"

"Very well, thank you." The young doctor seated himself next to Helene, smiling around at the other guests. "Kept busy," he went on, "but I wouldn't have it any other way."

"Of course," simpered Mrs Pendleton. "Doctor Kemp has a perfectly *wonderful* helper in Miss Proctor. Really wonderful! She's been with the hospital for years . . . "

"By the way, Jason," interjected Simon, with an apologetic look at Mrs P. for interrupting. "Didn't Miss Proctor come with you?"

"She'd just washed her hair, or something," he smiled. "Said to give you her apologies and that she'd drive over one day and meet your niece."

"I'll look forward to it," smiled Fenn, looking at the dark young man, at the dark hair, unruly and in need of a barber, the grey eyes and thin brown face that spoke of years in the tropics. His square jawbone gave him a sombre look, but at this moment, his eyes resting on the flushed and animated face of the beautiful Helene, he had none of the surliness he had shown to Fenn that afternoon.

She heard Mrs Pendleton asking how the latest crop of malaria patients were doing, adding, "I know for a fact that the doctor and Miss Proctor go for days without sleep . . . "

Suddenly, as if aware of Fenn's interest, Jason directed his gaze towards her and smiled. He said, speaking, she knew, to her and no one else in the room, "We're having quite a lot of babies born just now. One in particular, a bonny girl, born just before I left, in fact, she was the reason why I was late, for which I apologize, Simon, was a difficult birth, but is doing well, I'm glad to say." Fenn felt a warm glow spread through her at the news.

"Jason's wasted in this place." Helene's voice held derision. "I've told him time and again that he could do so much better for himself if only he'd make up his mind that he can. There are so many smart hospitals and clinics that would be only too glad to have someone as gifted in tropical diseases as Jason."

"I would not wish to work anywhere else." Jason's voice was quiet, almost bored, as if he'd been over the subject before and was no longer interested.

When it became time for the Pendletons to leave Helene yawned and said she too had better be getting along. They walked outside in the pale moonlight and Bill, who during the evening had said little but whose eyes were constantly on Fenn's face, said, "Would you like to come with me to Chubi, Fenn? Anytime, tomorrow or the next day. Whenever your uncle can spare you."

"Fenn's on holiday, Bill," her uncle reminded him. "She's a completely free agent to go and do whatever she wants."

"Where, and what, is Chubi?" Fenn laughed.

"It's a very beautiful part of the country where tea is grown. There are some lovely plantations there and we know quite a few of the older families."

"Fenn would be bored to death," Helene protested.

"No, I'd love it," Fenn smiled. There was much discussion on the interesting places Fenn ought to see and she finally said with a laugh, "How long is your vacation, Bill? You'll need a couple of months to fit all that into a timetable."

He smiled at her. "For you, my love,

I'd gladly give up my studies and make your happiness my sole concern."

She felt a blush sweeping up her face and looking round met Jason Kemp's amused gaze, which, to her dismay, made her blush all the more. Before she could say anything Angie came over and said, "Do ride over and see me, Fenn. You can tell me all the latest titbits from overseas. Here we hear nothing until its so old its no longer interesting."

"Of course. I'd love to. I'll give you a ring first."

After the last red tail light had dwindled down the driveway and into the night, Fenn walked with Frank in the garden for a last breath of cool night air before retiring. "Well, what do you think of Doctor Kemp, the poor old thing who prefers to live in solitude?" asked Frank with a smile.

Fenn grimaced. "You should have warned me. I thought he was about 75, at least, something on the lines of Doctor Schweitzer. And, of course, meeting him like I did this afternoon . . . "

She paused and Frank looked at her enquiringly, so that she had to tell him everything that had happened; the old woman, the girl, and her meeting with the doctor. Frank grinned widely. "Yes, he can be a bit of a tartar at times, can our Jason, but I'm afraid he's no stickler for convention so we just take him as we find him. Helene seems to be the only one who can get anything out of him."

"How do you mean?"

"Well, you notice how his manner softens when he's with her? Few people can do that to Jason. I've seen very small children do it, but few grownups."

Much later that night Fenn lay awake, trying in vain to sleep. It was partly the excitement of meeting new people, the heat of the tropical night and, more than anything else, she suspected, the meeting with Doctor Kemp. Was he always that direct with people? Had he at first sight decided he didn't like her? It would seem so, for all the signs were there. A most annoying part of the evening had been Helene and her patronizing remarks. She had asked Fenn whole strings of questions, hardly waiting for the answers.

"What sort of work did you do in London?"

"It must be absolutely awful to have to catch buses and trains all the time, and that dreadful weather . . . !"

She closed her eyes, trying to obliterate from her mind the dark loveliness of Helene Starr and the way all the men in the room, including her uncle, had looked at her.

4

UNCLE SIMON was already at breakfast when she appeared the following morning. "I've got to go down to the lower field," he announced, as Fenn helped herself to coffee. "Frank's already there. It seems as though some of the boys had a little beer-drink last night and in the resulting jubilations two of them had an argument over some girl and got a little carved up. They lose their heads so easily whenever they've got a little home-brewed beer inside them."

It was almost noon when the jeep carrying Uncle Simon arrived back. Reclining in the back under a blanket Fenn could see a figure over which a girl crouched. Her shrill wailing paused briefly as she looked at Fenn, then the lamenting started once more. Uncle Simon was agitated. Fenn recognized the symptoms. To Fenn's question he said, "It's the man who was knifed.

Worse than I thought, poor devil. We'll have to get him to Doc Kemp. Blast, and I had such a lot planned. Wasted half a day already."

"I can drive him over, uncle," Fenn offered.

Simon looked at her doubtfully. "I don't know, Fenn . . ."

"Oh, please let me! I'd like to think I was helping and wasn't just a guest around the place."

"Well, I suppose you could get Frank to drive you, although he's got his hands full at the moment . . ."

She shook her head, firmly. "No, I refuse to let you disrupt Frank's day as well as your own. I can manage, honestly."

Simon grinned, defeated. "Just like your mother," he smiled. "Always could twist me around her little finger. Well, now, let me explain to Doc Kemp what happened and tell him I'll be over later to see him . . ."

Muttering to himself he went off to telephone Mluba Hill so that they would be waiting for Fenn's appearance. Driving the truck she slowly made her way to the hospital. It was a nightmare journey to Fenn. She was not used to driving so unwieldy a vehicle and added to this was the necessity to go slow so that the injured man should not be jolted. Every time she made a mistake with the gears she shuddered, imagining the jolting of the poor fellow in the back.

She reached the hospital at what apparently was a visiting hour. The scene was very colourful and gay and after she had explained to the Anglo-Indian nurse, whose name she had learned was Yasmin, and had watched sympathetically while the wailing young girl followed them into the building, Fenn strolled amongst the crowd of people, smiling at the antics of the children. They peeped at Fenn from behind their mother's skirts, eyes wide and curious and when she spoke to them they answered, politely, "'morning, Missus."

Most of all the babies on their mother's backs fascinated her. Some she could barely see, so well wrapped were they and she wondered how they could breathe. Others wore knitted bonnets, in spite of the heat, and peered at the world over the edge of a brightly coloured shawl.

Suddenly she saw the nurse coming towards her through the throng and went to meet her. The farm worker, Nurse Yasmin explained, would have to stay the night and maybe the next day, but while the madam was here, wouldn't she like to see the baby?

For a moment Fenn was puzzled, then remembering the nightmare drive of yesterday afternoon, replied she'd love to. In the long narrow ward the light was dim and subdued, the high white beds neatly lined against the walls and the dark faces on the white pillows smiled widely at Fenn and the nurse as they entered. The mothers all knew of the white madam who had helped old Susannah and her grand daughter. Indeed, it was said that if it hadn't been for the white madam, the baby, and, no doubt, the mother, too, would not have survived.

Fenn followed the nurse to where a radiant girl lay with her baby cradled in her arm, a beautiful baby, round, fat and shining. African babies are beautiful at birth, and this one was one of the most beautiful Fenn had ever seen. It sucked a stubby finger, eyes an almost colourless blue, and gazed solemnly at Fenn.

As they admired it, there were steps at the doorway and Jason Kemp came into the ward. He was wearing his white coat, a stethoscope round his neck and looked very cool and competent. He showed no surprise at seeing Fenn there and came to stand with her and the nurse, looking down at the baby.

Fenn murmured a cool, "Good afternoon," to which he replied, "Glad to see you are taking an interest."

He spoke to the mother, in her own language, calling her Jessica. She heard him out, then lowering her eyes coyly, peeped under the sheet and answered softly. Jason laughed.

"What's your first name?" he asked abruptly. "I've forgotten, although I know your uncle introduced us."

"Fenn . . . why?"

A quizzical lift to one eyebrow. "Odd! Original, anyway. She wants your permission to name the baby after you."

Fenn flushed with pleasure. "Tell her

I'd be honoured! And tell her next time I come I'll bring it something — some clothing, maybe."

"She'd be very pleased. These people have so little and the children come off worse every time."

"What about her husband? Won't he be looking after her?"

She saw the nurse smile and turn away, and Jason lifted that eyebrow, saying, "She isn't married. She isn't even sure who the father is. Oh, don't look so shocked! These things happen even in the best of societies and even more so here. The Missionaries have taught them a lot but not yet how to avoid temptation."

Fenn frowned. "What will happen to her?"

"She'll wait until some man asks her to marry him, the grandmother said something about an older man whom she'd known since she was a child and who at one time was very keen on her. Whether he will still want to marry her now is another matter, but usually they don't mind too much about illegitimate children. The more hands they have to work in the fields the better they like it."

"Everyone says that about them," remarked Fenn, somewhat heatedly. "I think its a perfectly horrible way to regard children, as just another pair of hands."

Shrugging, Jason bent over the mother, saying something to her and Fenn noticed, irrelevantly, his eyelashes. They were very long and thick . . .

"She wants me to tell you," he raised his eyes and looked into Fenn's, startling her, "that she will never forget all you have done for her and the baby."

Piqued at herself she felt tears come into her own eyes and hoped he would not notice. He did not appear to for as he walked with her back down the ward he said, "The nurse did explain about the farm worker you brought for treatment? About his staying?"

She nodded, blinking rapidly as they emerged into the fierce sunlight. It was almost like a physical blow, glaringly bright after the cool dimness of the ward. "Yes, I'll explain to my uncle. I'm sure he won't expect him to return to work until he's quite recovered."

She felt suddenly very stiff and formal

with him, after the close intimacy of the ward . . .

A deep voice called across the dusty grounds. "Doctor Bwana! The Donna asks if the young madam will take tea!"

At Fenn's enquiringly look, Jason explained. "You haven't met Miss Proctor yet, have you? Come along and meet her. And I'm sure you'd like a cup of tea."

"I'd love some."

He led the way across the clearing where the shadows of the flamboyant trees made intricate patterns on the red earth. Fenn looked up into the spreading trunks of the trees. The leaves, green against the vivid blue of the sky against which the miniature flame coloured flowers showed exquisitely formed, like tiny orchids.

Jason led her up the half dozen cement steps, stained red and polished assiduously by Jason's houseboy every morning. The verandah, as at White Waters, stretched across the front of the building, shaded by creepers of bougainvellea and golden shower.

There were chairs grouped about a table and Jason pulled one out, a basket weave chair with brightly coloured cushions. "This is something of a surprise, Doctor Kemp," she told him as a white-clad servant placed a tray on which a heavy silver teapot and hot water jug struck sparks in the brilliant sun. "I never expected to find so civilized a spot in the middle of nowhere."

"Thank you," he replied with a small mocking bow. "Mluba Hill might not be Guy's, but we have our standards."

"I — I didn't mean to sound patronizing," she said, quickly.

"I'm sure you didn't," he assured her. "There are thousands of hospitals and small clinics about this vast continent, staffed by doctors of all colours and creeds. There are also thousands of holidaymakers who insist on looking down their noses at us."

Fenn flushed. "I don't look down my nose at you," she told him hotly. "Why should I?"

"Don't you?" he smiled. "The spoilt young niece of Simon Chase, bored with her life in London, looking for new kicks . . . "

"My uncle may be well-off, but I assure you I definitely am not . . . "

58

They glared at each other with open hostility now. A hostility that had probably been there since their first meeting.

"My uncle invited me to visit him for six months and I don't intend to sit and do nothing in that time. I shall help in any way I can."

His smile was twisted. "Good for you."

Fenn took a deep breath but before she could think of a suitable answer they were interrupted by the appearance of a small greyhaired woman in a blue cotton dress. Jason jumped to his feet, his smile suddenly warm, and made the introductions. "Fenn, I'd like you to meet Miss Proctor, — Amy, Fenn Adams, Simon's niece about whom I'm sure you've heard."

Miss Proctor was a small rosy-cheeked woman, her eyes as blue and guileless as the African sky in May. Her hair was set with an old-fashioned wave that dipped over one eye and thought she had probably worn it like that since she was a girl. When Fenn came to know her better she confided one day that she had never particularly enjoyed living in

Africa, but, strong as the call of her own north country moors and lakes, the ties that held her to her patients were even stronger.

Now Jason sat on the low wall with his back to the garden and watched as the two women took stock of each other. "Miss Proctor needs someone of her own sex to talk to," he said at last. "I hope you will find time to visit us often." Their conversation of five minutes ago might never have happened. Fenn realized Jason had called a truce and was quite prepared to play along with him.

He searched in his pockets, pulled out a pipe and proceeded to fill it. Miss Proctor looked at Fenn curiously and asked, "Fenn? What a lovely and unusual name, my dear. Do tell me how you got it!"

Fenn laughed, aware of Jason's eyes, still slightly mocking, on her face as she talked. "My mother and father chose Norfolk for their honeymoon and apparently there was a stretch of marsh land near the hotel where they stayed. The local people called it a fen. My mother said afterwards that she had been so happy there that when I was born just a year later they decided to call me Fenn."

"A lovely idea," smiled the older woman. "I like that! People are so prosaic these days, the world needs a bit of romanticism." Fenn heard Jason's low chuckle but declined to turn her eyes in his direction. Honestly, that man . . .

Later, they spoke of the clinic, of Fenn's life in London, of the problems peculiar to that part of the world. Especially of the hospital. It was a subject Jason thought much of, for he spoke with knowledge and ease. It was very pleasant, sitting in the deep shade of the verandah, listening to the deep voice of Jason and the soft lilting tones of Miss Proctor, watching the throng of Africans and their families talk and laugh outside under the trees.

The shadows were long, the sun low in the west when Fenn realized with a shock it was late. She stood up and held out her hand to the other woman.

"Thank you so much. Do you think I'd be in the way if I came again? Oh, not too soon or too often, but just occasionally."

"And why not? Perhaps, if your uncle does not object, we could find you something to do."

"Amy!" Jason sounded shocked. "Miss Adams didn't come out here to work . . . "

"But I'd love to help. Honestly!"

"So be it," he exclaimed. "If Miss Proctor can stand you under her feet, who am I to interfere?"

"Oh, take no notice of him," smiled the other woman. "Helene Starr is the only other woman allowed in these holy precincts."

When the young doctor had gone, answering a call from the nurse, Fenn, glancing shyly at Miss Proctor, said, "Miss Starr didn't strike me as being the type to be interested in this type of work."

"She isn't. But she *is* interested in Doctor Kemp." She gave Fenn a woman to woman smile. "What did you think of her?"

"She's extremely attractive."

"That's an obvious fact. I mean, what did you think of her as a person?"

Fenn considered. "She's very charming. I imagine she's an outgoing type, enjoys parties and the social life she's able to take part in, a fortunate person drifting along in a world made smooth for her by her grandfather's money."

"Very good, Fenn. You have a discerning eye for one so young. Then why, oh why, must she set her sights on our Doctor Kemp and . . . " She shook her head, breaking off in the middle of the sentence but adding, softly, "Remember, sometimes the packaging is so lovely it can be deceptive." She sighed. "It would be such a pity if Jason was enticed away after he's worked so hard to bring the hospital to its present standards. It's only now that the Africans are beginning to trust us. They didn't at first, you know. They ask for miracles, but they don't expect to spend any time here or submit to examinations."

"But surely, if Doctor Kemp wants so strongly to stay at Mluba Hill, Miss Starr cannot force him to go?"

"I doubt if anyone, including Helene, could force Jason to do anything he didn't want to do, but love is a funny thing. Men will do anything for a woman they love." There was resignation in her voice. "I'm very much afraid Jason's days here are numbered."

That evening Bill phoned to ask if Fenn would like to visit the tea plantation at Chubi the following day. "It's such lovely weather," he explained. "Who knows how long it will last. It seems such a pity to waste it."

"Love to, Bill," she agreed. "I'll look forward to it. What time do you want to set out?"

"About eight-thirty. It's quite a drive and its wise to get on our way before the sun gets too hot."

As promised, Bill arrived early, before the sun started its climb into the blue sky. Driving the red two-seater sports car he looked fresh and very handsome in the lightweight safari suit, fair hair shining in the early sunlight. After greeting Fenn and her uncle, he said, "No sign of rain! The weather man's really on my side, eh?"

"It's very good to offer to show me the countryside, especially on your vacation like this," remarked Fenn, climbing into the small car. She smoothed her skirts over her slim legs, aware of the open admiration in Bill's eyes. She had on a multi-coloured chequered shirt and a chinese yellow skirt, made of linen, with a bandeau of yellow silk holding back her dark hair.

Her uncle's eyes twinkled. "Oh," he said, "Bill, I'm sure, is only too eager to oblige — especially where a pretty girl is concerned."

"All too few of them around, sir, and your niece is one of the prettiest in a long time."

Simon Chase stood on the verandah and smiled benevolently as the car swept down the jacaranda-lined driveway and vanished behind the clump of bluegums that marked the main road. He wondered, idly, about Bill Paynter; about Helene and Jason Kemp and the sudden switch of affections. Bill and Helene had grown up together and everyone in the valley had taken for granted the fact that one day they would marry, thus combining the Starr and Paynter fortunes and the adjoining properties. Now, it seemed, Helene had other ideas.

And, as for Bill Paynter, well, Simon thought the world of Charles Paynter, Bill's father, but Bill had been involved in too many scandals, however mild they might have been, for Simon to think of him as a possible suitor for his niece's hand. He smiled at himself. Day-dreaming again! Fenn, he reminded himself, would not be here long enough to get involved with anyone, Bill or anyone else. But, he sighed, turning to go back into the house, wouldn't it be pleasant if she did . . . ?

Unaware of her uncle's thoughts, Fenn enjoyed her day out. Bill was fun to be with and anxious that she should enjoy all he had to show her. They left the car under the shade of a group of acacia trees and walked to the sorting shed where Bill knew the manager. An interesting hour followed, during which she was shown how the leaves were sorted and laid out to dry before being finally selected and packed into large wooden chests. The elephant, the brand of that particular plantation, was stamped on each chest and Bill ended his lecture with, "Now to Kwaaleni, our nearest town of any size, then the sea, eventually finding its way to dear old England and your local supermarket."

On the long drive home, the road ahead dusted with long purple shadows, the countryside about them took on all shades and colours. Finally they reached the turning for White Waters and as they came to a stop outside the house she noticed a beat-up old car standing under the jacaranda trees to one side of the verandah. Bill, noticing it at the same time, said thoughtfully, "I wonder what old Jason's doing here . . . ?"

The tall figure of the doctor appeared at the verandah door even as they spoke. "I was just about to leave," said Jason Kemp. "Just as well you arrived when you did. There's been a slight accident, I'm afraid . . . "

Fenn's face paled under its golden tan. Her uncle! His heart! Oh, no . . . ! "What is it?" she breathed. "My uncle . . . ?"

"You're uncle's all right, only he had a slight argument with a bit of tree-stumping machinery and the machinery came off best. Not as nimble as he used to be, the old man. He fell and if Frank hadn't noticed he might have been a lot worse, a whole lot worse . . . "

Fenn caught her breath, swinging her legs from the car as Jason continued, "He's all right. A bit shaken, but all right."

He stood aside as Fenn pushed her way passed him into the house.

"Fenn!" Bill's voice halted her and she turned to meet his questioning gaze. "Don't you even say goodbye? I thought you had enjoyed yourself?"

"I'm sorry, Bill, I have, truly I have. Thank you for a lovely day, but now I must . . . " Once more she turned to go, only to have him call after her, "I hope your uncle isn't too bad. Maybe we can do the same another day?"

"Of course. I'll look forward to it . . . " Not even waiting for the car to start she turned once more towards Jason. He was looking intently at her, but his eyes were mocking. Fenn felt the hot blood rush to her cheeks and she turned away abruptly. "I'd better go and see my uncle . . . "

Uncle Simon was sitting propped up against a pile of pillows and except for a flushed face and a bandage around his forehead, seemed little the worse for his mishap. Fenn stood near, a worried frown marring her brow and her uncle remarked, "Fenn, you look pale! Too much sun!" It was her uncle's voice that shook with concern. "It's not good for you. You're not used to it yet. I'll have to speak to young Paynter . . . "

"And why shouldn't I be pale? I come back and find you like this! You have literally hundreds of helpers on the farm and still you must try and do everything yourself!"

Simon's eyes twinkled. "Don't fuss, now. You're worse than Frank. You should have heard him! Anyway, enough about me. What sort of a day did you have with Bill Paynter . . . ?"

Now, with her uncle confined to bed for an indefinite period, Fenn realized that she was no longer a pampered guest but had already become an integral part of White Waters. The servants, warmly affectionate to their employer and anxious not to upset him by noise or worry of any kind, looked to Fenn more than Frank for smooth attention to their everyday problems, of which there were many and varied. She learned that the African is like a child, like a class of children, who, when the teacher is present works well and conscientiously, but let the same teacher leave the room for more than a few minutes and noise and horseplay is the result.

Frank, surprised that she was taking it so well, was grateful that she took the load off his own shoulders, thus enabling him to concentrate on the everyday chores of the farm. Bill phoned a number of times, begging her to find time to accompany him on more voyages of discovery, but each time she was firm and said, "Not just now, Bill, although I promise, as soon as my uncle is better, I *will* let you show me more of the district. I loved our day together and it shouldn't be too long before Uncle Simon is up and about again."

Bill, determined not to give up easily, especially now he had found someone like Fenn who, he knew, would only be with them for suh a short time, insisted, however, only to have Fenn declare, almost irritably, "Oh, for heaven's sake, Bill, I've told you I'll let you know."

Hanging up the phone she turned to find Frank's eyes on her, amusement — was it? — twinkling in their cool grey depths. "Doesn't give up easily, does he?" he commented, searching for his pipe in the large pockets of his bush jacket. "Helene was his all at one time. Now he seems to be questing for pastures new."

Why did everyone seem intent on pairing her with Bill Paynter, she wondered? Bill was a nice boy, pleasant and fun to be with, but she certainly had no intention of poaching on Helene Starr's property, either with Bill *or* Jason Kemp. The thought of Jason Kemp set her thinking about Mluba Hospital and Jessica and her baby, little Fenn. She had been unable to visit them for a number of days and when one morning she discovered a few balls of pale pink baby wool tucked away in a drawer which she was tidying, she was thrilled. Uncle Simon said her aunt had once intended to knit for someone's baby, but I believe she bought something instead. "You have it, dear, if you can find any use for it."

Find any use for it! Of course she

could find a use for it. She racked her brains for patterns and stitches, for it was impossible to obtain knitting patterns without driving into town, some sixty miles away, Fenn finally got down to knitting a matinée jacket and bonnet for little Fenn. There was enough wool to add a pair of booties and she had to laugh one evening while putting the finishing touches to the tiny garments, when she caught the look on Frank's face as she held them up, saying, "There, doesn't that look nice? I'm sure Jessica will be pleased."

Frank fumbled for his pipe, knocking it out on the empty fireplace, mouth twitching at the corners. "You'll be taking orders for the whole out-patients department, once they see that," he smiled, looking at her fondly.

The following morning, having been assured by her uncle that of *course* he would be all right for a few hours, besides, she needed the outing, she'd been stuck far too much in the house lately, Fenn saddled Esmeralda and rode over to the hospital below Mluba Hill. Miss Proctor was busy with a family of Africans who had just come in from the bush. Handing them over to Nurse Yasmin, she greeted Fenn warmly and invited her to tea.

Fenn laughed. "It's funny, but no matter what time of the day I come, its always tea time."

Miss Proctor echoed her laugh. "Don't then, make the mistake of thinking we do nothing but drink tea all day. Far from it."

"Oh, I know that, Miss Proctor. I was only joking. Anyone can see the amount of work, really valuable work, you and Nurse Yasmin, not to mention Doctor Kemp, do at Mluba Hill."

She had seen how well Miss Proctor and Jason got on together and their easy relationship as doctor and nursing supervisor made a great contribution to the efficient running of the small hospital in the bush. Miss Proctor had trained Nurse Yasmin herself, also, and the Anglo-Indian girl could be relied upon in any emergency. She held out the package in which she had wrapped the baby garments, saying, "I thought Jessica might like these for the baby. She seems to have so little . . . "

"My dear!" Miss Proctor unwrapped the tiny woollen garments with delight. "I'm sure she'll be more than pleased! Did Jason tell you we'd found a husband for her? No, of course you probably haven't seen him, not to talk to, anyway, since your uncle's accident."

That was true. He had been almost every day to visit her uncle but she was always in the kitchen, or the garden, supervising the gardeners, when he came, and there had been no opportunity to talk. Not that she would have gone out of her way to see him, anyway. Quite the reverse!

"Yes," Miss Proctor continued, not noticing that Fenn hadn't replied. "We've got Jessica a husband. He's much older than she is but I'm sure he'll make a good provider and give little Fenn a good home."

"I'm so glad," Fenn murmured, smiling, and looked up to see Jason approaching, a tiny kitten in his hands. He looked at Fenn then asked, unexpectedly, "Do you like cats?"

Fenn's eyes widened. "I adore them,

although I'm not too sure what Sean, Uncle Simon's red setter, thinks of them."

"This one's looking for a good home," Jason went on. "We managed to find homes for the rest of the litter but this little fellow has been left out in the cold."

Fenn looked at it, so small, so helpless, nuzzling its head against Jason's arm, crawling up his white shirt. No doubt it liked to be stroked by those strong brown hands, getting a sensuous pleasure from it . . .

Pulling her thoughts together, — Fenn, what is wrong with you, she scolded herself silently, — she said, "I don't suppose Uncle Simon would object and Sean's such an old softie he'd probably mother the creature. If — if you really want to give it away I'll be glad to take it."

"Splendid. I don't think for one minute your uncle will object but if he does you know where to return him. It is a 'him', by the way, not an' 'it'." His smile was teasing again. Was the man never serious, she thought.

He held the kitten towards her, and she took the soft furry body in her hands, touching one of Jason's for a brief moment. A kind of shock that was so disconcerting, went through her. She had to lower her eyes quickly, quickly so that he would not look into her's with the slight disapproval that his own grey eyes always seemed to contain. Flustered, she buried her face in the kitten's warm body, uttering soft soothing sounds to the small creature.

After a moment, during which time Miss Proctor busied herself with pouring fresh cups of tea all round, Jason went on, "Do you know how the farm worker is who was injured in the beer fight? We sent him home a few days ago but haven't seen him back for further treatment."

Miss Proctor sighed. "They seldom do come back. As I said before, Fenn, they expect miracles but won't come often enough to enable us to *really* help them."

Fenn stroked the kitten, now settling down on her knee with soft purring sounds. "It must be extremely difficult at times," she murmured.

"Disheartening is a much more apt word," Jason observed. "Still . . . " He gave a shrug and rose from his chair, preparatory to returning to his work.

"One tries. Isn't that all any of us can ever do?"

Fenn found herself looking at him in a new light. Maybe — maybe, she thought, the man was human after all. When it was time for her to leave they suggested she leave the kitten with them. Miss Proctor murmuring that she could not possibly manage it *and* Esmeralda, the mare, who this morning seemed more skittish than usual, prancing around in the dust in a most unseemly fashion.

Jason appeared to hold the mare's rein while she mounted. He stood for a long moment with his face tilted, eyes narrowed against the sun so that tiny wrinkles radiated from the corners of his eyes and the grey appeared a mere glint. He said, as soon as Fenn had got settled in the saddle, "I'll bring the kitten over as soon as I can. Don't worry about it, it's in good hands." For one ridiculous moment Fenn found herself thinking once more of those brown hands, with a fine scattering of black hairs on the back of the knuckles, and shivered. Observing the tiny movement, he said, almost anxiously, "You're all right, are you? Not cold?"

Cold, she thought? In this weather? "No, Jason, I'm not cold," she replied. Looking down at him, she smiled. Jason patted the mare's neck.

"Off you go, then, and try to keep Esmeralda in check. For such a mature lady she's raring to go this morning."

Back at White Waters she told her uncle about the gift of the kitten and he smiled and replied, "Fine, dear." Then he went on, "While you were out, Bill phoned and asked if you would like to accompany him to the club tomorrow. I thought a spot of swimming and lunch in the open would do you good, so I accepted for you. You don't mind?"

Fenn laughed and leaned down to hug him. "Of course not. Jason said you would be able to go about your business as usual soon and then *you* can take me swimming and for picnics in the open air. Do you the world of good."

Simon Chase gave her a fond look. "You like Jason Kemp, don't you?"

As she turned away, a flush rising to her cheeks, he continued, softly, "Jason's a fine man. The woman who marries him will get a prize."

Giving another, rather unsteady, laugh, Fenn said, "I wouldn't dream of arguing with you, Uncle, and I aon't suppose Miss Starr would, either."

He frowned. "Helene Starr? What has Helene Starr got to do with it?" Then, as light dawned, he added, slowly, "No, I don't suppose Helene would. She's had her sights set on old Jason for a long time. All the other men she ever was interested in capitulated at once, if that's the right word for it and I can't think of a better, and because Jason is a little more 'hard to get', Helene thinks he is the one and only."

Walking away, Fenn thought, Well, Helene had nothing to fear from her. Bill Paynter was much more fun and besides, she would not be here long enough to carry any entanglements to their rightful conclusion.

5

"YES," said her uncle next morning, "I'll be out of bed before you know it, and then back to work. I've been lazy long enough. That wasn't the way White Waters was born."

"You'll get out of bed when Doctor Kemp says so, and not a minute before," Fenn told him with mock severity.

His eyes twinkled. "Oh, bossy this morning, are we? Bill will have to watch out, I can see."

She wrinkled her nose at him and handed his breakfast tray to Daisy who had entered the room while they were talking. "But bossy or not, I must say Bill Paynter will be bowled over. You look very fetching this morning, if you don't object to an old man telling you so." Again his eyes twinkled. "Maybe that's the idea, though!"

Before Fenn could think of an answer the sound of a car outside was heard and her uncle continued, "Hurry along, then. Got your swimming things? There will be lots of young people there, always are during the summer holidays for most of them are with Bill at University. Enjoy your lunch. Serves a good meal, does old Don O'Brian . . . " Already he was lost in the sports page of that morning's newspaper.

"And who is 'old Don O'Brian'?" she enquired of Bill, laughing, as they left White Waters behind, the jacaranda trees pale in a sky still paler with heat.

"Manager of the Umzinpilo Sports Club," he grinned. "One of your uncle's old cronies. You're uncle has been quite a boy in his time. Believe they had some gay old times together in the early days of the colony."

Again Fenn laughed. "That I can believe."

★ ★ ★

They reached the club, turning off the main road along a narrow track lined with the beautiful orange/red flamboyant. The club house was a long white building with Dutch gabled ends. Everywhere there was colour; the fresh green of the smoothly cut grass on which figures in white bent over a game of bowls; the massed banks of brilliant cannas and multi-coloured beds of petunias in shades ranging from pale mauves to deep purple and yellow. Inside the blessed shade the long room had windows opening onto a screened verandah. Native made rugs covered the floor while comfortable chairs were arranged around low tables.

Bill took her by the hand and made his way over to where a group of young people sat under the deep shade of a tree, tennis rackets resting against their chairs, faces pink with the exertion of a hard game on such a hot day.

"Hi, Bill," they called on seeing him approach, and as one the men's eyes flew to Fenn. A number smiled appreciatively, while one of the girls murmured, "Hmmm, and who has our Billy boy found this time?"

As usual Fenn found herself answering questions, "What was London like?" and "Don't you feel madly bored living here after such a swinging place?"

Fenn heard herself answering, "I love White Waters, and I think you've got a wonderful country. I only wish you could parcel up some of this sunshine and send it home."

A blonde girl in a lacy white tennis dress, yawned and stretched. "You can have it. Sometimes its just a dam nuisance."

A young man grinned. "Lisa's mad because she burned her back so badly sunbathing yesterday she can't go in swimming today. Her own fault. She should know by now how much sun she can, and can't, take."

Bill said, "Talking about swimming, how about a dip before lunch, Fenn? We've plenty of time and you'll enjoy your lunch better."

Feeling extremely hot and sticky after the drive Fenn was grateful for the suggestion. "Sounds wonderful," she smiled.

"Good. Come on, I'll show you where you can change." With a brief, "See you lot later," to the group under the trees, who looked too lethargic to want to join them, anyway, Bill again took her hand

and led her to a row of wooden changing huts screened behind a long hedge of scarlet hibiscus. Some of the hut doors had tiny paintings of girls over them and Bill pushed her towards one of these, going towards one further down with a boy sign over it.

When she joined him a little later she made a neat compact figure in her one-piece yellow costume. Her dark hair she gathered and piled on top of her head, pulling on a white swim cap. After her time in Africa she was now attractively tanned and looking at her Bill pursed his lips in a silent whistle and grinning said, "Too much! You make Helene look positively skinny!"

"For heaven's sake!" she laughed. "Bill, you are such a fool! Come on, I'll race you to the other side of the pool."

Posing briefly on the side of the pool she made a neat header into the glittering blue-tiled pool, splintering the water into a hundred shimmering fragments. Laughing, he dived after her, surfacing a few yards in front, then with a strong crawl made from the opposite end, away from the groups of children who squealed and splashed at the shallow end. He reached it a few moments before she did, and watched with admiring eyes as she made the last few yards, laughing, shaking the water from her eyes.

"You cheated," she laughed. "You made a longer dive than I did."

"Okay, we'll do it again." Before she could stop him, he leaned forward and kissed her lightly on the mouth, then turned on his back and began a lazy backstroke. Like a golden fish, Fenn twisted and began to follow him. Half way across she realized he was no longer to be seen and she paused momentarily, her eyes scanning the surface of the pool for Bill's fair head.

Suddenly she felt cool hands grab her about the legs, pulling her down and she squealed, the squeal ending in a gasp as she went under. Water poured into her open mouth and she closed it hurriedly, seeing Bill's grinning face before her. His fair hair floated about his head in the water. His arms encircled her firmly, holding her to him, his mouth pressed cool and hard upon her's. She could feel the whole length of him against her.

For a breathless moment they hung there, suspended in the cool clear blue of the water. She felt her lungs choking and began to struggle, pushing him away from her feebly but her struggles only seemed to make him want to hold her more tightly. At last, when she felt she could no longer hold her breath and wondered how he could possibly do so, he released her and as one they rose to the surface. Fenn gasped the warm humid air thankfully, blinking in the rich golden sunlight that brought tears to her eyes.

"I think that was most unfair," she told him when at last she got her breath. "I'm not such a strong swimmer as you."

He regarded her lazily, floating on his back, hands barely moving to keep him afloat. "But you liked it, Fenn," he grinned. "Go on, admit it! You know you liked it."

Without another word she turned and like a golden shadow swam away from him, her heart still palpitating after Bill's show of passion. Her own feelings had disturbed her. Surely she should not feel that way about a boy she had known only a few weeks? Besides, she had never been particularly attracted to Bill's type, considering them far too highfalutin' for her taste. Oh yes, Bill was fun to be with, but if he thought she was a girl out for a good time who did not particularly care how she got it, well then, he was in for a shock. Never exactly a prude, Fenn held the thought that when she loved it would be a long, lasting love, a love ending in marriage and anything in between must therefore be superficial and transient.

Now tremulous and shaking she gathered up her towel from the blue mosaic floor that edged the pool and crossed to where the grass under the shade of a large tree looked cool and inviting. Planted there for that very purpose, the tree cast deep shadows upon the grass and Fenn spread her towel, seated herself upon it and pulled off her swim cap. Her dark hair, glistening like a raven's wing, fell to her shoulders and raising her arms she ran her fingers through it, sitting straight and tall, small breasts thrusting under the yellow swimsuit with her movements.

Bill came over and threw himself down beside her. Fenn half turned away, avoiding his eyes which laughed mockingly up at her. After a moment, when she did not say anything, he rolled over on his back, face up to the sun, eyes closed against its brilliance, and said, "Oh, all right, if that's the way you feel about it, I'll ask your permission next time." Eyes still closed against the sun's rays, he awaited her reply.

Fenn felt slightly foolish. After all, it had only been a kiss. Many a boy had kissed her, or tried to, on the dance floor, behind the filing cabinets in the office, in a taxi on the way home from a date. She had accepted them gracefully, but coolly.

Now, gazing down at Bill as he lay at her side, she smiled and leaning towards him said softly in his ear, "Sorry, Bill I admit to being childish. It was just that you — well, you surprised me, that's all."

His eyes opened with a snap. "You admit to being childish, then? Don't you also admit to enjoying it? I couldn't possibly mistake your response, Fenn."

He gazed up at her, minute drops of water still glistening on his skin, fair hair ruffled like a small boy's over his forehead. Before she could think of a reply he had drawn her towards him, so that she lay across his chest, his hands clasped lightly across her back.

"Bill . . . " she began, her voice sounding slightly breathless.

"Bill . . . " he mimicked, and kissed her again. She lay quite still, realizing that Bill in this mood was not a man to be trifled with. The kiss would be over in a moment and then she would make good her escape . . .

A voice above them murmured, "Oh, I *do* beg your pardon. I seem to have arrived at the most unopportune time . . . "

Swiftly Fenn sat up, one hand going to her throat. Through a haze of golden sunlight dusting the branches that hung above them, she saw Jason Kemp. He stood above them, derision — was it derision? Fenn wondered — in his eyes. He looked very cool and collected in a pale safari suit, long stockings that reached just below the knees, and tan suede shoes.

"I'm most terribly sorry," he went on.

"I had no idea . . . I have a message from your uncle, Miss Adams. He said I might find you here."

Fenn stood up quickly, clutching the white yellow bordered towel to her midriff, trepidation making her heart thump at his words. Her face paled, imagining Uncle Simon hurt again, imagining — oh, all sorts of things.

But Jason was saying soothingly, "Don't panic, its only a message. He said would you, Bill," his gaze now on the reclining Bill, eyes once more closed against the sun, "would you mind calling on Major Pendleton on your way home with Fenn? You have to pass the place and the Major promised to return some books he borrowed from Simon."

Bill smiled and lifted a hand in lazy assent. "A pleasure, old boy. I'll do that little thing."

"I'd do it for you," smiled Jason, his eyes on Fenn, mocking, ironical. "But I don't happen to be going that way." Then, giving the merest suggestion of a bow, he added, "Once again my apologies for, ahem, disturbing you both.

If you'll excuse me, I have things to do. Good morning!"

Fenn felt her face flame at the implication his words conjured up. She gazed after his retreating back, for once in her life speechless. How dare he? Just who did he think he was, anyway? Just because he had all those fancy letters behind his name did not give him the right to be so disparaging about Bill Paynter and herself. From behind the waves of anger she heard Bill's voice saying, "Come on, Fenn, I was just beginning to enjoy myself."

She felt his hands pulling her towards him again. Abruptly she moved away, wrapping the towel about her hips, sarong fashion. "No, Bill, I'm starving. Didn't you mention something about lunch after our swim?"

Rising to his feet in one swift motion Bill leered in comic fashion, hands curled like talons, reaching out for her. "So am I, m'dear, starving. But not in the way *you* mean."

By now his fooling was beginning to irritate Fenn. Now that her anger had cooled a little she wondered about Jason

91

Kemp, wondered what he would think of them, coming upon them in such a — compromising position, although it happened to be perfectly harmless. She felt, for his age, Bill could do with being a lot less adolescent.

She said, beginning to walk away, "Well, if you want to play games all day, I certainly don't. I'll buy myself lunch . . . "

He ran after her, grasping one arm just below the elbow. "All right, you win. Let's change and then I'll buy you lunch."

Towelling herself vigorously in the tiny wooden changing room Fenn tried in vain to keep from her thoughts the look on Jason Kemp's face when, at his interruption she looked up to find him gazing down at them. She felt herself going hot at the memory. Well, whatever Jason Kemp thought was no concern of hers, she told herself defensively. As for Bill, she was attracted to him but she didn't trust him. He was the kind of man who would find it extremely difficult to settle down with one woman. Each time a new girl appeared on his horizon he would be off in pursuit.

Feeling more irritated now than ever she joined Bill outside by the pool and they walked back to the clubhouse, Bill silent, not a bit like his usual gregarious self. But by the time they had joined the group of young people under the trees, the men leaping to their feet at Fenn's approach and pulling more chairs from adjoining tables, Bill was laughing and talking, once more the life and soul of the party. The talk turned to the native dances that were to be held in a few days time. It seemed that this was one of the big events of the year and Fenn sat quietly eating the delicious cold chicken and salad that the club provided for its members and their guests. She listened to the plans being made as to who should share who's car and had to smile at some of the bickering that went with the discussion. The blonde girl in the lacey dress looked at Fenn and said, "I suppose Bill will be taking you!"

Fenn hesitated. "I'm not sure. I don't know yet if my uncle will be fit to travel. He had an accident, you know. It wasn't bad but he did have to stay in bed for a while. Maybe Frank Telfer will take me."

"Frank!" Bill laughed, almost scornfully, and Fenn felt the irritation start up again. "Frank's got no thought for anything except that farm of your uncle's. I doubt very much if *he* will go to the dances."

The blonde girl giggled, reaching across the table to help herself to a tangerine which she peeled slowly then leaned back in her chair and smiled at Bill. "The farm, — and Angie Pendleton," she remarked, popping a piece of the fruit into her mouth, the juice running down her chin.

"Lise!" Bill looked at her warningly. "Don't gossip. It doesn't suit you."

Fenn, her attention caught, looked at them both with interest. Angie! What, now, had Frank Telfer to do with Angie? As far as she, Fenn, could make out, Frank regarded Angie as a rather spoiled child, gauche and immature.

Changing the subject, Lise said, "Has Doc Kemp been visiting your uncle, Fenn, or Miss Proctor?"

"Doctor Kemp," Fenn replied. "He's been extremely helpful and I must say

I appreciate all he's done, knowing how busy he is kept at the hospital."

"Talking of Jason," remarked one of the gang, quite casually, "didn't I see him here at the club a short time ago? Quite a surprise. He never favours us with a visit, must be something in the air."

Knowing looks had been exchanged at Fenn's remark of being kept busy at the hospital and before she could think up an answer as to his visit of a while ago, the blonde girl went on, "Yes, well, busy at the hospital but busier still courting our glamorous Helene. I realize 'courting' is an old-fashioned word," holding up one hand at the sounds of raillery that came from the rest of the party, "but I can't, at the moment, think of a better. Can you?" turning to Fenn, her green eyes taking in the flushed skin of the cheeks and forehead, where the sun whilst swimming had caught her, the slight frown between dark brows that told of a slight uneasiness at the turn of the conversation.

Fenn gave herself a mental shake and returned the blonde girl's smile with one of her own, equally cool, equally impassive. "No, I think the word 'courting' is very apt, in the circumstances. I must say they would make a very handsome couple. Any idea when the wedding is to take place?"

At this remark the group laughed out loud and a red-haired young man said, "That *would* be the tip of the year." The badinage grew to such an extent that Bill finally said, "Oh, shut-up, you lot! Have you nothing better to do than discuss other peoples affaires all morning?"

Surprised that he should take it so much to heart, Fenn gazed at him, a perplexed frown on her face. Before she could speak, though, the red-haired boy went on, scoffingly, "I know you and Helene had a thing going at one time, Bill? but I thought that was over long ago. Don't tell me you still care!"

"Of course I don't still care, idiot. Anyway, what's it to you if Helene chooses to go out with Jason Kemp or the King of Timbuctoo? She's a free agent, isn't she?"

At that the laughter became so uncontrolled that club members from tables nearby looked over curiously.

"Very free," laughed the blonde Lise. "She . . . "

Bill stood up abruptly, beckoning to Fenn. "I've had enough of this. Ready to go back, Fenn? Unless you want to stay here and listen to these — these morons."

Fenn too rose to her feet. "No, I'll come with you, Bill." Wondering about what had made him so angry, for they had only been pulling his leg, even she could see that, she said goodbye to the still laughing crowd and followed Bill back to the car park where his car stood under the shade of the flamboyant trees. He drove down the dusty track and back to the main road at a speed that had Fenn clutching the sides of her seat more than once. Finally they turned off along the driveway leading to "Masasa Ridge," the Pendleton's domain.

The Major handed Fenn the books on agriculture, asking her to tell her uncle "thank you," they had been extremely helpful.

"Always something new cropping up in farming," he smiled at Fenn and the silent Bill. "Think you know it all and then something happens that really throws you." Speaking to Bill he went on, "Had any trouble over your way, Bill, with this blasted army worm? I wonder if your grandfather . . . "

Fenn turned away as Angie appeared through the door leading to the verandah. "Fenn!" she called, delightedly. "I was wondering when you would come and visit me." Taking Fenn's arm she smiled and said, "Let's leave these two old farmers to their problems of farming and come into my bedroom. I'll get Cornelia to bring some lemonade. Or would you prefer tea?"

Fenn assured her lemonade would be fine and followed the other girl to a bedroom decorated in pink and white. It looked the same, she imagined, as when Angie had been ten or eleven. Even her dolls were still in evidence on the pelmet above the long windows. Angie saw her looking and said, eagerly, "Do you like it? I think it's a bit babyish but at least it's a place of my own where I can be alone."

"I think it's lovely," Fenn replied. She accepted the tall glass beaded with moisture on the outside which contained the home-made lemonade Mrs Pendleton was justly proud of, and seating herself upon the pink covered bed began to tell Angie about her morning, omitting the episode in the swimming pool.

Angie said, "I used to go the club a lot at one time but it gets such a fag seeing the same old people all the time. I hear you went to Chobi with Bill, too?"

"Yes, Bill's been sweet, giving up an awful lot of his time to show me the sights. Everything in this country is interesting."

"You won't be saying that in another six months," Angie warned.

6

AS the days passed, Fenn realized one thing. This life was spoiling her for the one to which she would soon have to return. Or, indeed, for any further travel. A few days later there was a letter from a girl with whom she had been friendly at Mr Hoy's waiting for her on the breakfast table.

"It's raining," she read, "Nothing unusual, I know. In fact, it seems to have done nothing else since you went away. I've been kept pretty busy at work, the old man moaning and groaning what a good helper he lost when you decided to leave! so haven't had time to do much visiting, but the few friends I have seen all send their love and say hurry back. Even Mr Hoy, believe it or not, says he misses you . . . and I don't think he just means workwise . . . "

Fenn folded the letter and laid it alongside her plate. Daisy approached from the sideboard with the silver coffee pot. "More coffee Miss Fenn?"

Fenn shook her head. "No thanks, Daisy, I've had enough."

The little maid smiled. "Mr Simon is coming to take his breakfast with you today. The doctor said he could get up."

He entered the dining room with the aid of a stick and Fenn rose hurriedly to help him to his chair. She settled him comfortably at the table then went round to resume her own place. "How are you feeling?" she asked, smiling.

"Grand! Never could abide staying in bed. It's wonderful to be up and about again."

She frowned with mock severity. "But not too long. Jason says . . ."

"Poof! Who cares what Jason says." His eyes rested on the letter Fenn was placing back in its envelope. "Letters from home, love?"

Fenn nodded, and leaned over to pour him some coffee. He buttered a piece of toast, carefully spreading the yellow home-made butter with a silver knife. "Makes you feel slightly homesick, eh?"

He placed the butter knife beside the

cut-glass butter dish and looked across to her, his eyes serious. "You know if you ever want to leave White Waters, return to your friends, you have only to say so, Fenn. I wouldn't dream of keeping you here against your will." He sighed, his eyes far away. At that moment the telephone rang. Fenn lifted it and heard Angie's voice.

"You haven't told me whether you're coming to the dance Fenn. I wish I had a car of my own then I could drive over and visit you, but Daddy won't let me have one yet. He's terribly old fashioned. Says I must wait until I'm twenty. I suppose he doesn't trust me or something."

"Well, the roads *are* pretty bad, Angie," Fenn told her soothingly. "I know how he must feel. And you'll be twenty in no time, won't you?"

"Next May." Angie's voice took on a brighter tone. "Anyway, Fenn, what about these dances? Mother said to ask you to come with us, and of course you must. I know, to your sophisticated ears, it doesn't sound much, but believe me it is. We have a super dance afterwards at the club near where the dances are held and sometimes don't get home until morning. You absolutely *must* come. I won't enjoy it one bit if you don't."

Fenn hesitated. "Well, Angie, as you know my uncle hasn't been very well, although he is up again now. Still, I wonder . . . ?"

"Nonsense. Frank, who *never* comes to the dances, by the way, too involved in his work, the old wet-blanket, *he* can look after your uncle. But I bet he insists upon you going, once he knows we've invited you."

"Who, Frank or my uncle?" smiled Fenn, still not used to Angie's inconsistent way of talking.

"Your uncle, of course."

At lunch she mentioned the conversation to her uncle who she thought was looking much better, more alert and attentive after his morning's work with Frank. "Of course you must go," he said, smiling at her across the table. Frank, tucking in with gusto to the strawberries and cream presented with such finesse by Ellias to tempt her uncle to eat, looked up and nodded his assent. "Don't worry about Simon. Go and enjoy yourself. The dances are held once a year only, you won't get the chance of seeing them again. They are something to do with the Gods of the local people. It seems they must be held only in November, when the moon's at a certain point. Extremely interesting. I vouch you won't find anything like them in London." He smiled, showing he meant no offence by the remark.

"Well, if you're sure," Fenn murmured. "I have no idea how long we'll be away."

"Liwani, where the dances are held," Frank told her, "is just over a hundred miles away. I realize that seems an awful long way to go to see Africans dancing, but in this country it is nothing, and they do put on a most magnificent show. Almost frightening, some of the more war-like dances. Anyway," he added, reaching for the silver coffee pot, "you can always keep an eye on Angie."

Fenn gazed at him curiously. "Why should I keep an eye on Angie?" she wanted to know.

Her uncle laughed. "Oh, Frank still

thinks of Angie Pendleton as a little girl. I think if he had anything to do with it she'd still be at school."

To her amazement Frank blushed, quickly lifting his napkin to his mouth in an effort to hide it. "Well, you tell me when she's grown up," he muttered. "In my opinion, as Simon said, she should still be at school. At least it would keep her busy. You know the old saying, 'The devil makes mischief for idle hands?' There isn't enough for a girl like Angie to do in this valley."

"Maybe," Fenn began, "if she could meet a nice boy she'd get married. I imagine Angie as the mother of a brood of children. She seems so much to want to love, and be loved, by someone."

Frank gave her a look that made her wonder what it was she had said wrong. Then, murmuring his excuses, he left the room.

Fenn turned to her uncle, eyebrows raised in query. Simon Chase smiled and said, "I cannot understand why Frank gets so riled whenever Angie Pendleton is mentioned, but, by gum, he does. You'd think, at times, that Angie had done some dreadful thing to him, but knowing Angie since she was born I know that's impossible. Angie's a delightful child, wouldn't hurt a fly."

"You see, even *you* think of her as a child. I imagine she might resent it, at times."

"Nonsense. As I said, Angie's a delightful child and nothing else."

Major Pendleton always referred to himself as a gentleman farmer. On retirement from the army he had purchased a small farm some little way away from Simon's and carried out mixed farming. Green lawns flourished right up to the walls of 'Msasa Ridge', so called because of the grove of lovely measa trees on the hill behind the house. A few days after Angie's telephone call Frank drove her over and after a few sundowners, explaining he couldn't stay to dinner much as he would have liked to, he left, admonishing Fenn to enjoy herself and on no account worry about her uncle.

Later she followed Angie from room to room, from house to garden having the dam and orchard pointed out to her with the promise of seeing them on the morrow in daylight, for the short twilight of Africa had passed and the sky was already a velvet curtain of ebony. As they prepared for bed Angie began to talk of her parents and her life on the farm. "It's all right at times and I love Msasa Ridge, I wouldn't want to live anywhere else, but . . . " and she fell silent, staring into the moon-drenched garden.

"But . . . ?" prompted Fenn, smiling.

Angie picked at the corner of a blanket. "Well, shouldn't I be thinking of marriage and babies? I mean, I'm nearly twenty. I can't wait for ever for some man to come riding up on a white horse and whisk me away. Besides, how would he ever find me, hidden away on this farm, miles away from anyone . . . ?"

In spite of herself Fenn had to smile at Angie's fears at being an old maid at 'nearly twenty.'

"He'd find you." Fenn's voice was very gentle. "He'd find you somehow, Angie. Don't worry."

But the younger girl continued to look worried. "I mean," she went on, "I'm not even the sort of girl men like . . . "

Now Fenn had to laugh. "What on

earth do you mean?"

"I'm the kind of girl who gets taken to football matches or asked to pass the tools while he changes a flat tyre. That suits me. I do far better on the back of a horse or driving a tractor than trying to behave like a little lady at some tea party. For instance, look at Frank, — and Bill, in a way Bill's sorry for me and Frank still thinks of me with pigtails and with braces on my teeth."

Fenn's smile widened. "I'm sure he doesn't, Angie. You're a very pretty girl. I know dozens of girls who would give anything for your skin and those big brown eyes."

Angie brightened immediately, looking at her in the semi-darkness. "Do you really mean that, Fenn, or are you just saying that to make me feel better, not so much of a tomboy?"

Fenn reached over and pressed the small sun-tanned hand. "You'll see."

Early next morning, long before breakfast, there was a spate of telephone calls, one in particular from Bill saying he would definitely be there.

"Watch out for me, Fenn," he said, his

voice deep and husky. "I would not miss a day out with you for the world."

Fenn laughed and promised she would. Shortly afterwards Helene, accompanied by of all people, Jason Kemp, arrived, Major Pendleton hurrying forward to greet them with delight.

"You managed to come then after all, Jason! *So* glad you did. We see so little of you these days."

His wife came over, followed by a white-uniformed servant carrying a picnic basket, which was placed in the boot of the Pendleton's large roomy car. Angie explained, "We always picnic by the river on the way over. It's a long drive and no point in taking it all in one gulp. Besides, the river's beautiful. I'll show you my favourite places . . . "

Breaking off she gazed across to where her parents were talking to Helene and the young doctor and murmured, "Well, well, so dear Jason has seen fit to come after all! Wonders will never cease."

"Doesn't he usually?" Fenn wanted to know. Angie looked amused. "Never before, but then Jason's long been the exception proving every rule in this place. Seldom relaxes. That's why I'm so surprised he's taking a whole day off from his beloved hospital to join us."

The two girls gazed at the young doctor and beautiful girl talking to the Pendleton's and Angie added, "I suppose Helene's coaxed him into coming this time. Everyone must relax occasionally, even Jason Kemp."

Fenn thought of the thin intelligent face, the cool grey eyes. He certainly did not look like a man who needed to relax. He looked as though he was doing exactly what he wanted to do with his life — and would continue to do it regardless of opposition, Or maybe, *because* of opposition . . .

Helene was holding Jason's arm, gazing up into his face with all the assurance that her perfect beauty gave her. Oh well, she thought, moodily, we can't all be perfect . . . The drive, once they started, included some of the most beautiful scenery in the valley.

Later Angie said, "I adore this drive," as they stopped by a bend in the river for the lunch time break. Flowering gum trees dipped over the river's edge and

Fenn could see pink and white water lilies floating at the side of the water where it was stilled by a natural barrier of rocks. The two girls sat together and sipped luke warm orange juice from a bottle and endeavoured to eat their lunch before the myriads of ants arrived.

"When I was a little girl," Angie went on, "this drive was the highlight of the school holidays. Bill was always home and we'd dare each other to cross the river by those stones," pointing a slim brown finger to a line of boulders made frighteningly slippery by slimy green moss. "Once, I remember, Bill got across and stood prancing and making faces at me from the other side and not to be outdone I managed to get half way across and then lost my nerve and Frank, who happened to be with us on that occasion, had to come over and drag me back."

She pulled a face, wrinkling her nose comic-fashion. "He did just that, too. Literally *dragged* me back. I was twelve and absolutely furious, as you can imagine."

Fenn laughed. "Yes, I can imagine, all

right. At twelve we consider ourselves very grown-up and responsible."

"Frank, though, still treats me as twelve." Angie added, frowning. She plucked dejectedly at a blade of grass and thrust it between her lips eyes gazing unseeingly across the stretch of oily green water.

To change the subject, Fenn said, "What did your parents think? I mean, you trying to cross the river? It looks extremely dangerous."

"They, of course, thought us absolutely mad. They still do, especially Bill." Fenn thought of the irrepressible Bill. Then her thoughts, without her bidding, flew on to Helene — Helene and Jason. Where were they? Helene's red car would be terribly conspicuous on the flat veldt country over which they travelled. And yet, although Helene and Jason had left almost immediately behind them, there had been no sign of it. Not even a dust cloud in the still air of the plains.

Continuing their way to the small mining village where the annual dances where held they passed groups of huts where goats, tended by native children with sticks, straggled across the road, making Major Pendleton curse freely and blow hard on his hooter. The Major parked the car in the dusty carpark, his good temper restored because he was able to secure a place beneath a group of shady trees. The sun burned down from a sky of brilliant blue, not the sign of a cloud anywhere. These had been left behind with the mountains. Fenn caught herself wishing it *would* rain. Just a swift shower to relieve this terrible oppressive heat. She mentioned this to Angie who looked sympathetically at her and replied, "I didn't think it was all that hot, Fenn, although I supposed I'm used to it. Sure you feel all right?"

Fenn gave a short laugh, murmuring that it was probably the long drive, coupled with the heat. She wasn't used to either. The wooden seats on which they were expected to sit, even if they were under a sort of canvas awning, could hardly be called the height of comfort, and in spite of, or maybe *because* of, the canvas awning, the sun continued to beat down on them like an open furnace. Fenn could feel her skin prickling with the heat and a thin film of perspiration covered her upper lip and forehead, tasting of salt when she explored her top lip with the tip of her tongue.

To her surprise Helene and Jason were already seated and the Pendleton's made a bee-line towards them. "Make yourselves comfortable," Jason smiled, indicating the row of empty seats below his and Helene's. "Plenty of room for everyone."

Once again she touched her tongue to her upper lip, and caught Jason's eyes, mocking, full of irony, and felt herself redden. "Why does he do this to me?" she asked herself. "Would it be better if I looked him straight in the eye and smiled right back?" This, she decided, she would do next time she caught him looking at her in that curiously deflating fashion. But when, in the excitement of the dancing, the noise and sheer dynamism of it all, she *did* catch him looking at her, she threw her head back and laughed still louder. To her surprise Jason joined in and beside her she heard Major Pendleton say, "My goodness, I haven't seen old Jason let himself go so much in a long time!"

Soon after this Angie's parents left for the Mine clubhouse. "We've seen this so many times," Mrs Pendleton explained, touching a tiny cambric handkerchief to her brow, "that I really do think I would rather wait for you young people in the cool of the clubhouse. It really is so terribly hot."

"Of course, mother," exclaimed Angie, waving a negligent hand. "We can look after ourselves, can't we, Fenn? Besides, Bill should be here before long. He can drive us over to the club."

The dancers stamped and turned, spears held high and threateningly, gleaming in the bright sunlight. Their shields were made of cowhide; white and brown and black. They had strings of beads and feathers tied about their ankles and the ground shook to their stamping.

"I know one thing," observed Angie, after one particularly frightening bit of leaping, "If I'd seen them coming towards me, screaming and jumping like that, there wouldn't have been this particular member of the Pendleton family as a pioneer!"

Fenn laughed, and a voice behind them said, "Well said, young Angie. I can imagine, after seeing this, many a member of our older families would think the same."

Jason sat behind them, smiling. Of Helene there was no sign and he explained her sudden absence by saying, "Helene found the heat too exhausting and has gone on to the club with some friends."

When the last of the dancers filed from the arena, Jason said, "Well, that was really something. Who's for a long cool drink?"

Angie jumped to her feet. "Come on, Fenn, Jason's taking us for a drink."

Fenn hesitated. "Maybe we should wait for Bill," she suggested.

"Nonsense," scoffed Angie. "If he wants us he'll know where to find us."

"Of course, if Fenn would prefer to wait," Jason began, looking at Fenn with that mocking glance that made her blood come near to boiling point.

"I think I will, if you don't mind," she said, coolly. "You go on, Angie. We'll join you later. Bill can't be far away, I'm sure."

"I'm sure he can't," murmured Jason. With another mocking smile he left, holding Angie lightly under one elbow, guiding her across the maze of wooden seats.

Fenn sat and seethed. For heaven's sake, where *was* Bill . . . ? She looked round and saw him coming towards her, stepping over the seats as though in a great hurry. "Fenn, I'm so sorry! I ran into two blokes from the University and couldn't get away. They insisted on buying me a drink and I've missed all the dancing . . . You look tired, darling," his voice suddenly taking on a worried tone. Let's get you under some shade and a few cold drinks inside us."

From the look of him he'd had enough drinks, Fenn caught herself thinking. Nevertheless, this and the 'darling' she chose to ignore and taking the hand he offered followed him across the banks of seats. At least, she told herself, Bill was a man who showed his feelings and did not try to bury them under a smooth exterior and mocking eyes . . .

They drove in Bill's car along a bumpy dirt road. The sun was fast setting in the west, long shadows falling across the road in front of them. Bill was driving very fast and Fenn wondered if drink had this effect on him and just how far this clubhouse was. She sat inflexibly in her seat, her back and head aching, thankful when at last they reached the clubhouse gardens. The driveway was crowded with cars of every age and description. The sound of laughter and music echoed into the darkening day and Bill pulled up with a shriek of brakes, in a hurry to join the merrymakers.

"We always have a whale of a time," he grinned, helping Fenn from the low seat of the car. "Usually end up with a champagne breakfast."

"Sounds fun." Fenn had never been to a party that ended with a champagne breakfast. She wondered, idly, what it entailed, but did not want to risk Bill's laughter by asking. She gazed at the crowd of cars parked seemingly haphazardly before the wide verandah. "There seems to be an awful lot of people here," she murmured, to which

Bill replied, "And how! One of the events of the season. The next big 'do' is at Christmas. Come on, I'll introduce you to some people you'll like. My kind of people."

Inside the clubhouse the girls were mostly in terrace gowns. All were deeply suntanned and looked energetically healthy as they jived around the floor to the music of an African band, seated on a small raised dias at one end of the long room. "It's the Native Police Band," Bill told her. "Always get them to play on this occasion. Jolly good, too, considering it isn't really their kind of music."

Fenn might have argued with him there. The music, to her humming ears, sounded definitely African inspired, drums thundering out their jungle-like messages, saxes high and shrill, glinting silver in the light from the coloured lanterns overhead. She felt a slight dismay at the sounds and bustle all about her. The nagging headache which had been bothering her all afternoon was beginning to get her down and she wished there was some way she could escape from all this, gay as it might prove to be, and return to the peace and solitude of White Waters.

The day had been long, starting early as they did, almost before sunup. She could only suppose these people were used to it, the bumpy, dusty journey, the unshaded seating arrangements, and now this, the sort of event which at any other time she would have enjoyed tremendously but now felt it was all too much for her.

"I'll get you a drink," Bill said in her ear. "What would you like?"

Before she could answer someone called to him and he vanished in the mêlèe of people around the bar and Fenn was left to stare after him, hoping he wouldn't get her too intoxicating a drink, hoping Angie would appear and rescue her, perhaps have some aspirins . . .

Next to her a girl was complaining, "My housegirl *ruined* my dress. I had to wear this one. Dreadful, isn't it?"

Fenn glanced at the offending dress, a heavy silk caftan in shades of orange and scarlet, and thought it looked very nice. She looked down at her own. No one had thought to advise her about bringing a long dress for the dance at the club afterwards and she felt rather out of place in her own thin frock, pretty as it was in shades of peacock blues and greens.

Bill returned holding a couple of glasses and handed one to Fenn.

"It's quite innocuous," he grinned, Seeing her hesitation before sipping the drink. "Lime and a tiny spot of gin, with lots of crushed ice. Alright?"

Fenn nodded. The drink was certainly refreshing, trickling past her parched throat with the coolness of a mountain stream. She smiled brightly at Bill. "Tell me who everyone is," she forced herself to say, determined to enjoy herself, and if she did not, at least try not to spoil *his* fun.

Bill looked about him vaguely. "Well, there's the group you met at the Mlingwe Club, that day we went swimming." He grinned at her, in a conspiratorial way, bringing back clearly the lighthearted, sun-filled day, Bill's kiss under the water and her own embarrassment at Jason Kemp's sudden appearance. "Then," Bill went on, "over there I can see Helene and old Jason, having a whale of a time together. There's one thing about our

Doc Kemp. When he does come out of his shell, he surely knows how to enjoy himself, especially if Helene happens to be around."

Fenn looked, then turned her head away quickly at the sight of the lovely dark girl and the young doctor dancing together. One brown hand was laid lightly, but, it seemed to the watching Fenn, so positively in the middle of her waist. His dark head bent over hers and Fenn saw her look up and laugh gaily at something he said. She closed her eyes against the absolutely gorgeous terrace gown of wild pink, orange and green, with wide flowing sleeves that Helene wore. She looked alluring and sexy, the gown cut almost to the thigh on one side, the neckline so low her skin showed deeply tanned . . .

The babble of the conversation, coupled with the sound of the band seemed to fill her head and suddenly Fenn wanted to get away, away from these rather exotic people, to be alone, all by herself, for five minutes . . .

Gazing up at Bill, she said apologetically, "Bill, would you mind awfully if we go outside for a while? I — I feel — rather groggy. I've had this headache all afternoon . . . "

Immediately Bill was all concern. "My dear girl, why on earth didn't you say so? I don't want you to pretend you're enjoying yourself if you really don't feel up to it."

"No," she protested. "I was enjoying myself, really. But this headache is getting more than I can bear . . . " She sighed. "Perhaps a breath of fresh air might do the trick."

"Certainly, old thing. Would you like me to get Helene, for you, or Angie . . . ?"

Fenn bit her lip. No, certainly *not* Helene, she thought. "If Angie has some aspirins on her," she murmured, "maybe she'd let me have one. I don't seem to be able to get rid of the headache."

"You're bid is my command," he joked, but his eyes showed how concerned he really was. "I'll go find Angie, but first let me get you comfortable on the verandah." He led her out onto the verandah, deserted now but for a silent footed servant collecting empty glasses from a table nearby. His white uniform gleamed in the darkness and he gave them a friendly grin before disappearing through an open door further down the verandah from where came the sound of soft laughter and the clink of glasses being washed.

There was the light sound of footsteps and Angie's voice behind her exclaimed, "Bill tells me you're not feeling well! Is there anything I can do, dear?"

"I've got a headache, Angie, that's all. I asked Bill to ask you if you had anything on you for it."

Before she had finished speaking Angie, with a slight laugh, burrowed in the tiny pink-beaded purse she carried. "Bill made it sound as though you were at death's door, to say the very least. Scared the life out of me. Here, love, a couple of aspirins. Shall I get you some water?"

Fenn nodded and watched Angie walk to the open door of the kitchen and call something in the native dialect. Almost immediately she reappeared with a glassful of water and Fenn swallowed the tablets thankfully. She placed the glass on an empty table and seated herself on top of the low wall surrounding the verandah. "Now, take it easy," Angie advised. "I wouldn't go back to that racket just yet. Terribly noisy in there."

Fenn nodded without speaking, feeling the tight band of pain across her temples already beginning to fade. She took a deep breath of the flower scented night air. "I don't want you to miss the dancing, Angie. Leave me. I'll join you and Bill later."

"Wouldn't dream of it," Angie replied, lips tightening. She seated herself next to Fenn, swinging her legs and gazing out at the dark and silent club gardens. After a moment, she said, almost hesitantly, "What brought all that on, anyway? I mean, one moment you were enjoying yourself with Bill, I could see you across the room, the next you were doing a vanishing act with him."

Fenn stared at the speck of light made by a firefly hovering over a bush of fragrant gardenias just below them in the garden. "All what?" she hazarded, knowing full-well to what Angie referred.

The other girl made an impatient gesture. "You know, your headache! You should have mentioned it before. My mother's very good at headaches. In the summer her life is just one continual headache. The heat affects some people that way."

Fenn thought back over the events of the day. The slight ache above her eyes had assumed jumbo proportions only when Jason and Helene had danced by . . . Once again she caught herself thinking of Helene in that wonderful striped concoction of filmy silk, almost transparent in the bright lights of the clubhouse. At the way her glossy hair cascaded down her back, Jason's hand entangled in its silky strands, almost caressingly . . .

For heaven's sake, so what, she scolded herself. Both Jason and Helene were free agents. It seemed to be taken for granted amongst the various farms in the valley that they were intended for each other. In a few months she, Fenn, would be gone from here, forgetting all these rather hot-house people.

To change the subject she asked about Angie's partner, a rather gauche young man she had noticed her dancing with.

Angie wrinkled her pert nose. "Oh, Tommy Evans, you mean! He's a bore! I've known him since I was a kid. Can't talk about anything but farming."

Fenn smiled. "Well, after all, farming is what most people do around here, isn't it?" And, she told herself, from what she had seen of their houses and cars and swimming pools, farming was definitely a paying proposition.

Angie went on moodily, "I know, but we don't want it rammed down our throats all the time, do we? Helene, now! I envy the way *she* lives. She's hardly ever here, travels all over the place, has a terrific time."

Fenn said, curiously, "Hasn't she any parents? I've never heard about them."

"They divorced when Helene was still a child. Her father works somewhere in Brazil, building bridges or something. Her mother re-married, an Italian Count, and lives in Italy."

She gave Fenn a sudden astute look. "Helene's had as a beau just about every available man in the valley. Bill was going steady with her for a while, then suddenly something seemed to happen and Bill wasn't around anymore. Jason took his place. But for all that, whenever Bill appears, you'll see Helene give him the old sweet smile she now reserves for Jason."

Headache now completely forgotten, Fenn looked at her. "What, both of them at once?" she asked, surprised.

Angie looked at her pityingly. "Helene collects scalps, love. It's her favourite hobby. As Bill isn't around so much these days, University and all that jazz, and Jason is, Helene is busy trying to collect him. I tell you, she isn't a girl to be trifled with. She's always got everything from her grandfather, and the more hard to get the man is, the more Helene is determined she will get him."

"But how does Jason feel?" Fenn asked, frowning. "Surely he can see what a flirt she is."

Angie shrugged. "He's a reserved type but certainly does come to life whenever she's around, and old Jason doesn't do that easily. So go carefully with both of them, Fenn. I've noticed how Bill is attracted to you, and Helene doesn't encourage anyone to trespass on her reserves, past or present."

Suddenly Fenn recalled how angry Bill had become that day at Mlingwe Club when they had began discussing Helene and Jason. She sighed. Helene, as far as she was concerned, was welcome to them both. "In any case," she told Angie, "I won't be here long enough to worry about Helene's — or anyone else — lovelife." But she turned her head away as she spoke, not wanting Angie to see her face as she said the words. Her past life and friends seemed like something dimly glimpsed through a mist of yesterdays . . .

Just then Bill reappeared. "How's the old head?" he asked, smiling at the two girls. Angie turned on him accusingly. "Bill Paynter, were you listening just now?"

"Who me?" He sounded affronted but at the same time winked at Fenn. "Maybe a teeny bit. That's the only way I keep up with events in the valley, by listening to gossip." He grinned at Angie in the semi-dark. "That is an extremely interesting view you have of Helene and Jason. I must say."

Angie glared at him. "Don't you dare repeat it to anyone, you skunk, or I'll kill you."

Bill tut-tutted. "Really, such language from such a well-brought-up young lady." He turned his attention to Fenn, holding out one arm in a gesture of old-fashioned gallantry. "I think, after *that* exhibition, darling, we'll go in and enjoy ourselves."

Inside the music was as loud as ever, the colour and laughter of the dancers as clamorous, but now Fenn found herself beginning to enjoy it. Her headache had completely vanished and she told herself she must make up to Bill for her earlier lack of gaiety. Letting herself go, she proceeded to dance with all and sundry. A dozen different young men, all snared by the vivacity of this lovely stranger in their mist, clamoured for her attentions and before long she found herself facing Jason who had appeared as if from nowhere and was standing in front of her, smiling, giving every indication that he would like to share the next dance with her.

When he held her in his arms she was

astonished at her own feeling of warm response. The dark shadowed face above her seemed like that of a stranger, grave and brooding. What was he thinking about as he held her so close amidst the swaying crowd, so hemmed in by the other dancers, and yet so entirely alone?

"Enjoying yourself?" he asked, smiling down at her.

"Ummmmn, yes," she murmured, feeling much as that tiny kitten must have felt at the warm voluptuous feel of his arm about her. As if reading her thoughts, he said, "I haven't brought the kitten round to you yet, but I aim to do so in the near future. We've been terribly busy at Mluba Hill. In fact, it was only with the threats of Miss Proctor ringing in my ears that if I did not take time off to go to the annual dances and so get away for a day, I, too, would be added to her patients, that I consented to come. She has a knack of getting her own way, in spite of her white hair and kindly manner."

"I don't blame her," replied Fenn, smiling. She added, more seriously, "I feel quite guilty at not coming over to give her a hand lately. I didn't know you had been so busy."

His eyes twinkled. "I quite understand. You are here on holiday and an invitation to go swimming at the Mlingwe club with young Paynter is much more fun than helping at Mluba."

Fenn flushed but before she could think of a suitable answer she noticed across the room Helene glaring at them. Helene, whose lovely face at that moment was far from lovely, but malevolent, full of resentment. She stood and talked to a dark young man who was trying very hard to make the lovely girl notice him but even Fenn could see from that distance that he was wasting his time. The ache above her eyes began again, seeming to intensify and the throbbing beat of the drums seemed to merge with her heartbeat.

Suddenly there was a terrible rushing sound in her ears. The whole room spun in a kaleidoscope of colour and she felt herself sinking into a well of darkness. When next she opened her eyes she was lying on a leather couch in what was obviously the clubhouse office. Metal filing cabinets stood under the window and a typewriter stood on a desk nearby. A worried looking man in a dinner jacket stood near, glass of water held in one hand, eyes dark with concern. As she tried to sit up Fenn heard a voice, Jason's voice, murmur, "Lie still. You can sit up when I tell you to and not before."

His hand pushed her back against the cushions that supported her head. She lifted her own, a very shaky one, and pushed the tumbled hair from her brow. It felt as though a very tight band was bound firmly about it, just above her eyes, and she had difficulty in focusing them. Everything seemed blurred.

"What happened?" Her voice was as shaky as her hand.

But Jason was occupied in feeling her pulse, taking her other hand and holding it firmly in his, eyes fixed on his wristwatch. He gave a grunt, dropped her hand and looking down at her, one eyebrow raised in that sardonic fashion that so infuriated her, although somehow, now, it did not, he said, "You fainted, that's what happened. Care to offer a reason?"

Fenn lay back and gazed at him with wide eyes. He looked so tall, so virile in his white shirt and dark tie, (most of the men had removed their jackets because of the heat,) that it was difficult to associate him with the dour young doctor at Mluba Hill. Why, she thought dreamily, irrationally, the man is positively handsome . . . !

She said, her voice low and husky, "I've — I've had a headache all day and it seemed to get worse a little time ago. I thought, perhaps, it was the heat . . . "

"It's more than the heat," he told her, with authority. "You've got quite a temperature, young lady, whether you are aware of it or not. We're going to have to get you home and to bed. There are any amount of tropical bugs one can pick up in this country and you've obviously got one of them."

At Fenn's look of alarm, one hand going to her throat, he smiled, adding, "Not to worry, as our dear friend Bill would say. We'll look after you."

There was a sound at the door and

Angie came in, followed by her mother. The blonde girl's face was pale. Her eyes flew straight to Fenn, laying there, looking so wan and ashen that Angie caught her breath in a sob and ran forward, falling on her knees at Fenn's side.

Her mother, calm, very much the Major's lady, said, "Do stop acting, child. Fenn will not relish someone dripping tears all over her, not when she is so obviously indisposed."

Jason turned to her and said, "Fenn's got some kind of fever, Mrs Pendleton. I am going to suggest we get her straight back to White Waters and to bed. We can go in my car.

Through a haze in which there was heat and voices and the throbbing headache that persisted and persisted and refused to leave her, Fenn felt strong arms slide under her, lifting her and carrying her effortlessly outside. The noise of the band was left behind but now she could hear what sounded like Bill's voice, arguing, a monologue that went on and on, broken at last by Jason's curt tones that seemed to quieten him. Then she was sitting in a car and someone was sitting next to her, and the last thing she remembered was an arm going round her pulling her head onto a comforting shoulder . . .

She dozed and when next she woke it was to find herself in her own room at White Waters, with Selina clucking over her and Uncle Simon standing at the foot of the bed looking, as Jason was telling him, like "death warmed up."

"Go to bed, Simon. There is nothing you can do. Selina's more than capable and I'm going to give your niece something to make her sleep." There was the sound of her uncle's voice, "All right Jason, I might as well go back to bed if she's going to sleep."

7

WHEN Jason arrived the following day the weather had changed and the rain was coming down in torrents. The wind lashed it against the windows of Fenn's room, at times buffeting them with such fierceness that speech was almost impossible. The sky grew dark early that day, huge black clouds building up above the farm like bastions of the devil. But in Fenn's room it was warm and cosy, the pink-shaded bedside lamp casting a peach glow over her slim suntanned shoulders in their flimsy nightgown.

Jason felt her pulse, fingers cool and firm, eyes downcast to the watch on his wrist. He took her temperature and gazed sternly down at her at her request to get up. "I feel much better," she murmured. "My headache's gone and . . . "

He frowned. "Gone, has it? Are you sure?"

She lowered her eyes to the lime

green satin bedspread, fingers plucking at it impatiently. "Yes. I *said* it's gone, didn't I? How many times do I have to repeat it?"

She would have noticed his frown deepen if only she had cared to look up. "Temper! temper! Just because we are told to stay in bed for a day or two doesn't mean we must take it out on the poor old doctor."

She at last raised her eyes to meet his, flashing and defiant. "Stop treating me like a child, will you? I'm going to ask my uncle if I may get up and if he says yes then *you* Doctor Kemp, are certainly not going to stop me."

"There are heads and brick walls," murmured Jason, smoothly. "And beating one against the other does not help."

"I *will* get up," she murmured rebelliously.

He laughed. "You sound just like a woman."

"I *am* a woman."

"I know," he said. "I'm just beginning to notice."

There was the sound of a door opening behind them and her uncle entered to hear the end of the argument. He gazed at the girl in bed, a pained expression on his face. "My dear Fenn, don't tell me you are *arguing* with Doctor Kemp?"

"That surprises you, does it?" She turned her head to look at her uncle, dark hair brushing her bare shoulders. "I suppose no one ever *dares* to argue with the great Doctor Bwana?"

All the pent-up emotion of the last few days, the heat, the dance, Helene, came rushing back and she felt tears prickling at the back of her eyes. Turning her head away she was not to see the look exchanged between her uncle and Jason or the smile that accompanied it. Jason shrugged and said, "Oh, don't worry, a good many people take time out to argue with me, the Government, the hospital trusties, Helene's grandfather, as well as Helene herself. I listen, but I don't know if it gets them anywhere."

"Jason is the one man I know, apart from Frank," Simon Chase remarked, "who really knows in which direction he is going."

Fenn's eyes still avoided the young doctor's amused gaze. "How fortunate," she murmured. "To know exactly where you are going."

"Don't you, Fenn?" His voice was soft, serious now, all badinage gone. "Somehow you always struck me as being the type of modern girl who knows exactly what she wants out of this life and goes all out to get it. I remember your uncle told me you want to travel, and after you've finished your visit here you plan to move on and see what the rest of the world has to offer." She felt him move closer to the bedside and turned her head, to gaze up into grey eyes that looked down into her's, so close. So very close . . .

"Of course," she said, exasperation taking hold of her at the way those same grey eyes could melt away any resentment she might feel at his derisiveness. "Of course I know what I want to do. Doesn't everyone? After I leave White Waters I . . ."

"Don't let's talk about you leaving White Waters yet awhile, Fenn." Her uncle's voice cut in softly, startling them. It was all too apparent that the man and the girl had completely forgotten his presence, lost in a little world of their own making. "We intend to keep you here for a long time yet."

"*And* keep her in good health while she is here," smiled Jason. "And to that purpose I insist that your niece stay in bed for another day, at least. A fever can be a treacherous thing. You imagine, once the headache is gone, that you feel wonderful, but it isn't so. One more day, Fenn! Let's call a truce, eh?"

Fenn hesitated, then, more because her uncle was watching than for a natural reluctance to give in, smiled and nodded. "All right. But I assure you, Jason, I really *do* feel so much better."

"I'll be here first thing in the morning. If you still feel the same I promise you shall be allowed up then."

When next he came he brought her the tiny kitten he had promised her that day at the hospital. It snuggled into her arms as he handed it to her and she raised enraptured eyes towards him. "Oh, Jason, you remembered!"

"Naturally." His tone was faintly smug, making her smile widen as she buried her face into the kitten's soft fur. He went on, giving her that lop-sided grin of his, "As you come to know me better, you'll discover I always keep my word. Now, if you'll put that creature down for one moment I'll take your pulse and we'll see about you getting up."

Five minutes later, satisfied that she was indeed much better, her pulse and temperature normal, he straightened his back and grinned down to where the kitten was sharpening its claws on the lime green bedspread. Fenn gasped and made a grab for it, causing the bedclothes to fall away from her flimsily clad figure. There was a flash of golden tanned thighs, then she pulled the sheet and thin blanket that was all she needed in the summer's heat over her and, face reddening under his amused grin, said quickly, "How — how is Miss Proctor? It seems ages since I last saw her."

"Miss Proctor's fine," Jason replied, deftly untangling the sharp claws from the green satin bedspread. He held it on his knee, one tanned hand fondling its ears, making it arch its back and purr loudly in the still room. "She asked me to say how sorry she was she wasn't able to visit you but we really are busy just now at Mluba. This rain," — for it was still coming down in torrents and had been all day and the previous night — "is wonderful for the farmers, but it brings in its wake an awful lot of illness and extra work for us at the hospital." He sighed, a sound that caused her heart to skip a beat and then resume at a more rapid rate. "I think its harder to get them to admit they are sick and come in of their own accord than to actually treat them. Those that have spent some time at Mluba Hill and emerged cured are loath to return to us again. They have superstitious notions about the danger of entering hospitals and the odds against coming out alive. No amount of convincing can change their minds on that subject."

"How silly," Fenn observed, almost heatedly. "After all you have done for them."

"They are pleased with what we have done, but there is no word for gratitude in their language."

"Then don't you feel, sometimes," hesitated Fenn, knowing she must sound like Helene and hating it, "that you are wasting your time here? If they feel no gratitude for what you are doing . . . ?"

He shook his head. "Not at all. I chose to specialize in tropical bugs because they fascinate me. I like research and I enjoy the field work. The tsetse fly, especially. I've made a close study of that." He gestured with one hand. "This, as you might guess, is the ideal place for that."

There was a moment's silence while Fenn thought about his reply. Then she said, "You must be made of sterner stuff than me. I'm sure *I* would resent working so hard and so devotedly to receive so little thanks for my efforts."

"Oh, but we sometimes get immense gratification from our work. Look at Jessica and her baby, for instance, just *one* instance. Where would she have been without the hospital? Of course," smiling, "one Fenn Adams helped, too, by first bringing her to our notice."

"How is Jessica and the baby?" Fenn asked. "Have you heard from her since she left you?" Jessica, she knew, together with baby Fenn, had left almost a week ago to join her future husband at his village up country. Fenn had been so pleased that at last the girl would have someone to take proper care of her. The elderly man who was to marry her, according to tribal customs, Jason had explained, not in church, had promised to be good to her and care for the baby as though it was his own.

Conveying all this to Fenn now Jason smiled. "Although before many months are out there will be a playmate for baby Fenn, no doubt, and one every year until Jessica gets past child bearing. The Africans like big families."

"I — I don't know if I like that," Fenn murmured. "In fact, I'm *sure* I don't like it. It's one of the things I feel really strongly about."

"What, big families?" Jason sounded amused.

"No. I don't object to big families, if that is what the couple desire and they can afford them. But when they are brought into the world, just as an extra pair of hands, to help with the work, then I think its — its . . ." She searched for a word that would interpret her feelings on the subject, only

145

to have Jason offer, his lips twisting with amusement, "Disgraceful?"

Fenn felt her face go blank. "Now you are making fun of me again! Why is it that we cannot hold a conversation for more than a few minutes before you start being sarcastic . . . ?"

He placed the now sleeping kitten beside her on the bed and leaning over, to her consternation, dropped a swift kiss on her forehead. "For your information, my sweet Fenn, I wasn't being sarcastic. When I am, you'll soon know it. Now I must go. I've wasted enough of an all too busy morning talking to you already."

She gazed up at him with cheeks reddened. As though it was *her* fault he had stayed, she thought, with indignation. "And I *can* get up, can I?" she flung after him as he made to leave the room. He turned at the doorway, one hand holding the doorknob. "Yes, you may get up. But if you should feel in the least giddy, or your headache reoccurs, your uncle had better phone me. Although, knowing you, you probably won't even mention it." With that parting shot he was gone, leaving the lovely white and apricot room strangely empty. Fenn gazed at the closed door, seething at his remark. Never sarcastic, was he? Humph! Gently lifting the still sleeping kitten from its nest of green satin, she pulled the bedclothes up high under her chin. She snuggled back against the pillows, one hand holding the kitten to hollow in her neck. It moved and yawned, a tiny pink mouth with white pinpricks of teeth, and Fenn laughed. "You are beautiful," she told it. "And I must stop thinking of you as an 'it'."

★ ★ ★

It was the following evening that Ellias, the cook, came silently in from his kitchen and said, quietly, "There is someone outside who wishes to see the madam."

Simon raised puzzled eyebrows and looked at Fenn. "In this weather?"

Fenn turned to the waiting servant. "Who is it, Ellias? What do they want?" Then a thought struck her and she half rose from her seat.

"Is it someone from the hospital? Doctor Kemp . . . ?" No, of course not, she rebuked herself. Jason would hardly be likely to come to the back door. Frank said, in his slow, easy voice, "Why don't we go and see?"

He stood up, carefully placing his pipe on the red brick hearth, and followed the cook along the passage to the kitchen. The back door stood ajar and just inside, but not far enough to escape the drenching rain, stood Jessica. A dark woollen shawl was wrapped around her head and shoulders and Fenn could see where the baby was tied to her back beneath its sodden folds.

Alarm filled her and she ran forward, pulling the girl in by one hand, gesturing to Ellias to close the door behind her. "Jessica, what on earth has happened? Why are you out in this awful weather? And the baby, too?"

At her voice the African girl broke into heart rending sobs. She wiped one hand across her nose, tears running down the dark cheeks and gazed at Fenn with red-rimmed eyes. Fenn could see, against the dark flesh, a purple blue bruise, almost closing one eye. Turning to the old cook, Jessica went into a long-drawn out monologue which, after listening patiently to for a few minutes, Ellias stopped with a sharp word and in turn faced Fenn.

"She says, Miss Fenn, that her husband has beaten her and turned her out of his house. She wants to come and stay with the madam at White Waters."

Fenn turned desperately towards Frank and he said slowly, "I think our best plan would be to get hold of old Jason and see what he thinks. These people are funny. You cannot interfere in their family life . . . "

"Interfere?" Fenn almost spat the word. "I'm certainly going to interfere in *this* girl's life, Jason or no Jason. Look at her, Frank! How can you send her back to a man who does that to her? And the baby! For heaven's sake get it into something dry. Ellias, see to it . . . "

Later, in the lounge, Frank telephoned the hospital and spoke to Miss Proctor. She explained the doctor had been called away but that she would come over the following morning "May I speak to Fenn, Frank?"

Handing the telephone receiver to the

waiting girl, Frank rejoined Simon by the fireside and Fenn heard Miss Proctor's soft voice saying, "Jason intended to drive over and see you this morning, dear, but he was called away. However, I have strict instructions that I was to keep an eye on you but with the rain and all I just couldn't make it. How are you feeling, anyway?"

"I'm fine, but I'm terribly worried about Jessica and the baby. What will happen to them now, if her husband refuses to have her back?"

"Oh, I expect Jason will think of something. He usually does. Don't think me hard, Fenn. It isn't that. But there *are* places these girls can go, maybe a domestic school where they are taught housework and simple cooking. We could get her a position as a house servant if she could do that."

"I see," murmured Fenn slowly. Yes, maybe that would be the answer. "Then she wouldn't have to go back to that awful husband . . . " she added into the phone.

"Don't take these things too much to heart, child," Miss Proctor said softly.

"Maybe later you won't be able to keep her *away* from that awful husband. We don't even know what she *did* to warrant the beating. I've heard rumours that Jessica's quite a flirt, and these people have different ideas on that subject to what we have."

"Hnmmm . . . " murmured Fenn, thoughtfully, and hung up.

The following morning the rain had cleared, although, as her uncle said, gazing up at the sky with experienced eye, more wasn't far off.

"Good season," he murmured. "I know the continental rains can be the very devil at times, depressing, making everyone irritable, but its the lifeblood of White Waters."

Miss Proctor arrived shortly afterwards and followed Fenn into the lounge, pushing her soft white hair back from her brow, where the damp air and the drive over had made it flop. "Phew," she breathed. "it's certainly turned sticky again. I sometimes think the rain makes the heat more intense, like a heavy blanket pushing down on the world."

Daisy appeared with a tray of tea and

as Fenn poured the older woman said, "How's Jessica? If you like I'll take her back with me. She can help out at the hospital until she decides what she wants to do."

Handing her a cup and saucer Fenn said, "Ellias settled her in a spare room for the night and Daisy looked after her and the baby." She thought of the African girl's radiant face this morning as she greeted Fenn before breakfast, the plump gurgling baby in her arms, the misery of the previous night already forgotten. The warm sunshine of a new day put everything into a new prospective.

Fenn continued. "She seemed much better but she assured Ellias, that under no circumstances, would she return to her husband, so there's one of your theories gone for a loop."

Miss Proctor shook her head sadly. "I will never understand them, Fenn. She seemed so eager to go to him and he to have her. Maybe later, when she's thought it over, she'll change her mind. Still, Jason gave me strict instructions that I was to make sure you are fully recovered, so let's forget Jessica and her problems for the time being."

She produced a thermometer and disregarding Fenn's assertions that she felt fine, took both her temperature and pulse. Afterwards she smiled at the girl and said, "You'll do. Put the doctor's fears at rest."

Placing the thermometer back in its little silver case she went on, "He's been so busy. You've no idea. Just as I was leaving a procession arrived . . . " She paused, shaking her head sadly and at Fenn's frown of enquiry, went on, "Fenn, you should have seen them. Pitiful, the father near to death, the mother almost as bad, a baby that, heaven be praised, was all right, but the son, a boy of about thirteen, at death's door. Poor Doctor Kemp didn't know if he was coming or going."

"What was it?" Fenn, prepared for almost anything now, even if the answer had been bubonic plague, was amazed when Miss Proctor replied, "Measles."

"Measles?"

Miss Proctor nodded. "It takes a dreadful toll each year in Africa, believe it or not. The poor things haven't got the stamina, the resistance powers that we have." As she spoke her kind blue eyes clouded with hopelessness.

"When one member of the family gets the disease you can bet that the rest of them will come down with it, too. Sometimes whole villages go sick and then we hardly see the doctor for days on end . . . "

"Remember you promised if I could help in any way, Miss Proctor," Fenn reminded her, leaning forward, eyes shining. "And I know I had measles when I was a child so you've no problem there. There must be something I can do, even if its only bathing the babies."

They both laughed at the idea of Fenn bathing a baby, then Miss Proctor frowned, saying, "Well, an extra pair of hands never went wrong, dear, provided of course that you are quite recovered from your own illness."

8

LATER that morning Fenn was busy in the kitchen with Ellias when the sound of another car outside made her wipe her hands on a towel and go outside to greet who ever it was calling. Ellias had been showing her how he made the delicious strawberry jam for which White Waters was justly proud and Fenn found herself wishing that whoever was calling would not keep her long for Ellias lessons were most interesting.

Frank was out on the land inspecting any damage the heavy rains might have caused. Uncle Simon accompanied him, sitting by his side in the landrover, dire threats from Fenn ringing in their ears if her uncle was allowed to do too much. Wondering who could be calling her heart sank a little when she saw it was Helene, for, secretly she had hoped for Jason . . .

Getting out of a small imported car

that had obviously cost her grandfather a small fortune, she crossed the lawn with her usual gracefulness, looking absurdly lovely in a white dress that showed off her dark colouring to perfection. "Hi!" she called, coming up the red polished steps, swinging a huge white straw shoulder bag in one hand. She wore white sandals and no stockings and, as always, Fenn felt something definitely lacking in her own appearance whenever she saw this beautiful girl.

"Hello, Helene," she said, smiling a welcome, a welcome which she certainly did not feel. "Thought I'd drop in on you as I was passing," was Helene's greeting remark. Her next one surprised Fenn. "Seen anything of Bill Paynter today?" she went on.

Fenn frowned. "No. Was I supposed to?"

Helene lifted slim shoulders in a shrug and without answering came onto the verandah and chose a cane chair with high fan shaped back and gay cretonne cushions in which to stretch her slim, deeply sun-tanned body.

"Some, these days, I always connect

Bill with you," she drawled, digging into her bag and producing a thin silver cigarette case. "Rumour has it that White Waters is one of his favourite places."

"Rumour isn't always necessarily right," smiled Fenn, matching her own tone of voice to Helene's lazy one. The dark girl glanced sharply at her, eyes smouldering. She opened the cigarette case and produced a filter tip, then, as an afterthought, offered one to Fenn. At Fenn's shaken head she drawled, "of course, you don't indulge, do you! I don't suppose you can afford it, over there," making the words 'over there' sound as though Fenn came from the back of beyond.

Why, she wondered, did Helene persist in making ironical remarks about Fenn's own country, remarks full of derision and — almost — contempt?

"I've never particularly liked smoking," she murmured. "Although I have an open mind on the subject and certainly don't object to anyone who wants to."

Pursing her full red lips Helene gazed at her thoughtfully for a long moment, then said, "Well, that seems to be that on *that* subject, doesn't it? Anyway, as I said, I really came over to find Bill. The skunk promised to take me over to Mluba Hill sometime this morning to see Jason."

Wondering why she could not go on her own, Fenn said, "Would you like some tea, or coffee, Helene? I was just going to get Daisy to make some more."

Helene waved a languid hand tipped with plum-red nail varnish.

"By all means." She let her hand fall negligently over the arm of the chair, holding the cigarette with slim brown fingers, smoke drifting upwards in a white spiral. Over coffee, which Helene said she preferred, they talked of various things such as the heat, Helene called it this 'bloody heat', the recent rainstorm and life in the small community of the valley. Then looking at Fenn, a speculative look in her lovely eyes, she went on, casually, too casually, "By the way, that little fainting spell you threw at the club after the native dances was very effective, I thought. You certainly got Jason home a lot earlier than we had intended. I remember how indignant I was when I heard he was leaving because of you."

The speculative look become more pronounced. "I must say you made a remarkable recovery."

Fenn brushed a hovering fly from her cup and said, quietly, "Jason is an extremely able doctor. You of all people should know that."

"Extremely able," Helene agreed smoothly. "And of course when we get to Cape Town things will be so much better for him. He's put up with the most inferior equipment for years but there he will have all the most modern facilities. You can't expect them in a place like Mluba Hill."

She paused meaningfully. "My grandfather has influential friends with the Tropical Diseases Hospital there you know. As soon as they secure Jason a position that suits his qualifications, we will be off."

Fenn gazed silently at her. She slowly stirred her coffee and said, "Doctor Kemp will be missed in the valley. I'm surprised he has agreed to leave. He seemed very happy here and the Africans love him."

Helene shrugged. "So, what is he supposed to do? Stay in this stinking valley for the rest of his life? Don't forget this concerns me, too."

"I didn't realize you were engaged, Helene. I thought . . . "

Helene laughed, a high brittle laugh that made Sean, laying nearby in a patch of sunlight, lift his head and look over lazily, sleepily curious.

"Oh, we aren't officially engaged, but we do have an understanding. With all the coming changes we don't know when we'll have time to fit in a wedding. But," she smiled at Fenn, woman to woman, "Jason is an extremely patient man and I imagine he will leave that side of our future life to me."

Smug, thought Fenn, acrimoniously, so smug it was almost unbearable.

When Helene had departed, skidding down the dripping jacaranda lined driveway with impatient speed, she carried the silver tea tray to the kitchen where Ellias waited, eager to give the English girl her next lesson in making jam. But curiously depressed by Helene's words Fenn found herself unable to settle to anything and was pleased, in a way, when Bill's car appeared on the drive and parked where Helene's car had been a few minutes before.

Bill jumped out, calling, "Fenn! Fenn!" His eyes caught sight of her just inside the screen door and he came up the steps two at a time.

His hands took hold of hers and he said, eyes searching her face, "My dear Fenn, I've been so worried. I meant to come over and see you but my father chose that time to have sudden urgent business in town and I had to accompany him." He stood back a step, holding her at arm's length, relief on his face. "But you look wonderful! When Jason carried you away from the club that night I nearly went berserk . . . "

Fenn smiled. "Don't exaggerate, Bill." She disentangled herself from his light grip and turned away. "I'm fine now, really. These new medicines work wonders. Was your trip to town successful?"

"Umn, what? Oh, yes. We sorted things out." He grinned. "At this time of the year my father's life is one long crisis." Fenn joined her laughter to his. Then he said, "Seeing that you've made such a remarkable recovery and that it's such a lovely day after the rain and, last but not least, Helene is on the warpath, looking for me, although I can't for the life of me imagine what I've done, how about a trip to Mgena Plateau? Remember you promised to come with me ages ago!"

Fenn hesitated. Why not? The day was gorgeous. Why mope around an empty house with Helene's words ringing in her ears? Her uncle and Frank would not be back until dark and Ellias was more than capable of seeing to them. Why not accompany Bill?

Her mind suddenly made up she smiled at him. "All right. Wait while I change my dress and put some shoes on." In the house she normally wore 'slops', an Indian type sandal made of flimsy leather thongs. She ran to her room, calling on the way to Selina to tell Ellias not to bother with lunch, also to tell her uncle, in case he returned before she did, that she was out with the Bwana Paynter. Quickly she changed into a simply designed dress of olive, flame and white, sleeveless and low necked, then after a moment's thought adding a lightweight cardigan in case the rain started once more.

The Mgena Plateau, Bill explained, was famous for its trout streams and fir plantations. Situated some thirty-five miles away it was National Parks land and Fenn noticed African wardens in khaki uniform patrolling amongst the trees that fringed the side of the road. This road, as usual untarred, climbed steeply around the side of the plateau, twisting and turning in so dangerous a manner that Fenn's heart was in her mouth almost all the way. The journey, however, was worth it, for as the car, covered in a thin film of red dust, climbed the last hundred yards and finally emerged onto a wide flat space used as a car park, Fenn gasped with pleasure.

It was difficult to believe that this was Africa, the Africa of the valley and plains below, dry and dusty and torrid. Lines of fir trees ran in stately procession in all directions. Pine cones were everywhere, crunching under their feet as they walked. A narrow stream tumbled over smooth green-flecked boulders and Bill said,

"The plateau trout are a real delicacy. Have you ever tasted them?" When Fenn shook her head he went on, "Well, we'll have to remedy that. There's an 'olde worlde' type Inn at the foot of the plateau where the trout are a speciality. I'll treat you to dinner there before we go back."

Fenn thought it all sounded wonderful, for with the cool mountain air and the long drive she was feeling definitely more peckish than she had for a long time. But she added, tentatively, "As long as we're not too late back. My uncle . . . "

Bill grimaced. "Your uncle knows you are with me. You left message to that effect, didn't you? He won't worry."

The rest of the afternoon passed very pleasantly strolling between the towering dark fir trees, finding a spot comparatively free from ants amongst the ferns that seemed to flourish with shameless vigour alongside the icy streams.

Fenn discovered they were icy when she slipped off her sandals and perched perilously on a rock, dipped her foot into the clear water.

She withdrew it with a gasp, grimacing

at Bill's guffaw of laughter.

"It's *freezing*," she said, hopping back to where he sat, a highly amused expression on his face. He clicked his tongue in mock sympathy, and pulled a large folded white handkerchief from his top pocket. Unfolding it carefully, he said, "Shame, I should have warned you. The water comes from higher up the mountain and is the nearest thing we'll get to snow in this part of Africa. Here, let me dry your tootsies . . . "

Fenn seated herself next to him in the cool green ferns. "No, it's all right, Bill . . . "

Before she could protest further he had taken her wet foot on his lap and was drying it tenderly. Feeling slightly foolish, Fenn said nothing but allowed him to finish. Then, sensing the effect the feel of her cool flesh was having upon him, the solitude, for there was no sign of other people anywhere, no voices, she made as if to rise, saying brightly, "Thanks, Bill. Now your handkerchief will be soaking. Let's hang it over that branch to dry . . . "

But the drying of his handkerchief was

furthest from Bill's thoughts. Reaching up with one hand he grabbed one of her's and pulled her down again. She gazed at him with misgiving. "We ought to be getting back, Bill. We've come quite a way from where we parked the car."

Once more, mockingly, he clicked his tongue. "You think of the darndest things to stop me from making love to you," he murmured, and before she could protest further he had pulled her towards him, his arms going round her, holding her to him, firmly, permitting Fenn no opposition.

The sun filtering through the tall trees, the cool splash of the gently flowing stream beside them, acted like a soporific to Fenn, and Helene's words still foremost in her thoughts she allowed him to kiss her.

He gazed at her curiously when the kiss ended in a long sigh. He kissed her again and she murmured, "Don't, Bill, you're not being fair."

"Maybe not, but I'm enjoying myself," he said against her mouth.

Suddenly, irritably, she tried to push him away. "That's all you seem to think about, enjoying yourself. Don't you ever — *feel* anything? About anything?"

"At the moment you'd be surprised at what I'm feeling," he said, his lips moving against hers.

"Bill, for heaven's sake . . . !" His arms were hurting her, so tightly did they hold her, so that when voices were heard nearby he released her and they continued their walk, Bill glowering like a small boy denied some treat he'd long been looking forward to. Pine needles carpeted the ground here and made dry crackling sounds under their feet. Bill reached for and held her hand and as Fenn didn't have the heart to refuse they walked like that back to the parked car.

As promised, Bill took her to dinner in the Mountain Inn at the foot of the plateau, where they sampled the fresh water trout Bill had boasted of. Afterwards they had coffee on the wide verandah. They watched the lights in the valley spring up through the dwindling day light, the sparsely strung-out golden lights of the small town just below, the pin-point lights of the cooking fires lit by African women to prepare their evening meal.

Down once more in the valley the air was warm and humid in spite of nightfall and Fenn thought with longing of the cool bath she would have on her return to White Waters. A long relaxing soak, to which she would add that gorgeous French bath oil smelling of sandlewood . . .

But once more in Bill's car, driving at his usual high speed, the night wind fresh on her cheeks, blowing her hair behind her like some wild thing, she felt much better and almost accepted Bill's offer of a drink at the club before going home. But she decided against this, saying, "I don't think I should, Bill. Thanks for the thought, but my uncle might not like me being out too late after my bout of fever."

Bill sniffed, then grinned his usual amiable smile. "OK love. Perhaps another time."

Fenn returned his smile. "Yes, I'd love to." Then, hesitating, she added "I'm really grateful for all the time you're spending, showing me around, Bill, and

I'm sorry for that episode on the plateau. Please don't think that you don't appeal to me. It's not that. You do, strongly. That's one of the reasons I mustn't let myself get involved . . . "

"But if you like me, Fenn surely . . . " His voice held bewilderment.

"You forget I'm here only on holiday, that in another few months I will be returning to my old life. I *can't*, I must *not*, let this one get too much a hold on me."

"But that's the whole point! You don't *have* to return to England. Why can't you stay here, marry me?"

Fenn shook her head resolutely. "Don't tempt me. You never know, I might horrify you by accepting."

He gave her the sort of indulgent smile given by Uncle Simon when he thought she had been particularly foolish. "Silly girl! I don't make a habit of asking girls to marry me and the few I *have* asked have shown their willingness to accept only too readily."

Fenn gazed at him curiously. Of course there had to have been girls in his life before her. Bill Paynter was far too good-looking a young man to not have been involved with someone, and her thoughts flew back to Angie's words at the club dance the night she had been taken ill. Helene! Helene had been one of them and Angie's voice came back, saying, "Helene doesn't encourage anyone to trespass on her reserves, past or present . . . "

Perversely, she said, "What would you do, Bill, if I said, 'Yes, please, I'd love to marry you?' Be as I said, horrified, or delighted? Or, perhaps, regretful that I've accepted you?"

"Now you are just trying my patience. Of course I'd be delighted. I was engaged twice before, and once nearly to Helene. None of them worked out. I know my father and your uncle would be thrilled to bits and just think of the travelling we could do on their kind of money . . . "

"Why didn't they work out?" Fenn broke in on his words. "Helene, especially? You've known each other since children, haven't you? I should have thought Helene would have been the ideal wife for your father's estate."

Bill shrugged. They were standing

outside the verandah at White Waters still. Lights shone in the house and the soft sound of a radio turned low came from the lounge where Frank and her uncle would no doubt be sitting, tired after their day on the lands.

Bill answered her question with, "To be quite frank, Helene doesn't know *what* she wants. She loves the gay life and the valley holds little interest for her. Little interest, that is, except Mluba Hill, and even that, I guess, will pall in time."

Before she could stop herself, Fenn began, "But Helene's not staying in the valley, is she? She told me she and Jason were . . . " Alarmed at the way her tongue was running away with her, she stopped, gazing at Bill with wide eyes, while he said, "She and Jason are . . . what?"

Making a negligent gesture with one hand, she answered, "Oh, nothing, just something we were talking about this morning before you arrived. She came here looking for you, by the way. Did you know?"

That impudent grin replaced the frown on his face. "Yes, I knew. I'd half promised to take her over to see Jason, but Helene gets to rely too much on me. I thought I'd let her make her own way for once. Anyway, Fenn, we seem to have got off the track of whether or not you should say 'yes' to my proposal." He came nearer, reaching for her with both hands, taking her slim waist in a firm grip, pulling her towards him . . .

Tilting her chin with one hand, he gazed down into her eyes, eyes dark blue in the dim light of a clouded moon. He grinned. "You are going to, you know, whether you realize it or not. Marry me, I mean . . ."

Knowing that to struggle would only make him more determined Fenn let him kiss her. Then she broke away as a voice, Frank's voice, called from the top of the verandah steps, "Fenn? Is that you?"

"Coming, Frank." Gazing up at the still grinning Bill, she said, "I must go . . ."

He released her at once. "All right, but don't think you'll get away all that easily, my girl. Next time we meet we'll discuss it some more, eh? Did you know I was going away for a time? My father insists I take an extra course on farm management. I'll probably be away before Christmas. Promise you will keep me in your thoughts, though." Smiling her assent, she left him and ran lightly up the steps to where Frank stood just inside the screen door.

He said, "Was that young Paynter? He seemed very reluctant to leave, didn't he?"

Fenn returned his smile. "Very reluctant," she agreed, and went in to see her uncle.

The following afternoon as her uncle settled himself in his accustomed place on the verandah, where he would remain, Fenn knew, until Daisy brought the tea tray in at four o'clock, there was a telephone call from Miss Proctor.

"Jason has no objection to you coming over, Fenn, providing, if he sees you tiring, you agree to return at once to White Waters."

Taking Fenn's silence as acquiescence, she went on, "Perhaps you would like to ride over later? We could discuss the work you could do, although I'm afraid I cannot promise Jason will be here."

"I'm not coming to see Doctor Kemp, but to help you." Fenn made her tone brisk but at her end of the telephone the older woman smiled, the corners of her mouth lifting slowly.

Quickly, Fenn called one of the gardeners to saddle Esmeralda and changed hurriedly into the pale yellow silk shirt and tan jodhpurs that suited her slim figure so admirably. She mounted Esmeralda and trotted over to the verandah steps to call to her uncle, "I won't be long, dear. I'm just going over to Mluba Hill, to see Miss Proctor."

"All right. Just be careful to be back before dark. Esmeralda's a bit nervous of the dark."

With a smiled assurance that she would Fenn trotted down the long driveway towards the road. There were few blossoms on the trees now, the jacaranda season was almost over. She thought of next year, of next jacaranda time, when she would be — who knows where? For some unaccountable reason the thought today depressed her. In fact, she found herself shying away from it, as though it were an impediment to her happiness. Far more pleasurable was the thought that she was on her way to help Jason with his work, to do something really worthwhile.

She saw Bill as soon as she passed the clump of blue gums bordering her uncle's land, dividing it from the road. Esmeralda nickered and sidled nervously as the small car drove slowly towards them. Fenn leaned forward, laying a gentling hand on the mare's neck, murmuring, "All right, girl, all right."

"Hello, there, out for a ride?" Bill's voice hailed her as he pulled up a few yards in front of her.

"I'm on my way to the hospital. They seem to have an epidemic over there."

Bill's nose wrinkled distastefully. "Ugh . . . !" he muttered and Fenn had to laugh at the expression on his face. "Oh, it's only measles, but apparently it takes on the proportions of an epidemic out here."

"Well, it's still a lovely afternoon. How about returning the old nag to her afternoon slumbers and letting me take you! After all, you owe me something for turning me down last night, even if it is only a temporary situation."

Giving a sigh of resignation Fenn agreed. It took but a few moments to hand Esmeralda back to one of the stable boys and transfer herself to Bill's car. They drove for a while in silence, Fenn's thoughts with Miss Proctor and Jason, longing to arrive to help in what ever way she could, longing to . . .

After a while Bill turned his head to look at her, grinning. "You know, Fenn, somehow I can't imagine you at this nursing lark. Why, you of all people, do you feel you have to help?"

"I'd want to help anyone if they needed it, and I think at the moment Miss Proctor can do with any help she can get."

"Little Miss Nightingale herself! Helene was right about you."

Fenn glared at him. "Really!"

"Yes. She thinks you are another martyr type, cast in the same mould as old Jason, that you both need your heads examining for worrying so much about these people . . ."

Fenn said again, "Really!" This time her voice held a note that made him look at her more closely.

"Bill," she went on, "I'm warning you, this has nothing to do with anyone except Miss Proctor and myself. If I feel I can *really* be of assistance I fail to see what it has to do with anyone, including," she added, grimly, "Helene."

Holding up one hand in a gesture of surrender, he grinned, "All right, I get the message. On our way let's go and look at those old Mission ruins over there, on the other side of Mluba Hill. I've always wanted to show them to you and I'm sure your old doctor won't mind waiting a few minutes longer."

He can change so quickly, so abruptly, she thought, it almost seemed that for more than a few minutes at a time he was never the same man.

"Bill, I did promise . . . "

"So what? The hospital won't fall apart if you don't arrive within the next few minutes."

Fenn sighed and got out of the car when he brought it to a halt at the foot of the green hill on which the hospital was built. To argue with Bill when he was in this mood would take longer than humouring him. They left the car parked under some trees just off the road and he led her towards the crest of the hill. The path, barely discernible in the tall yellow grass, became narrower as they walked and once Fenn stumbled over a half-hidden rock. Bill took her by the elbow, muttering, "Mind how you go . . . "

They walked in silence for a while, then he said, gazing at her curiously, "You haven't said much. Not mad at me, are you, darling?"

"No." Fenn did not feel like continuing the subject so turned her head away to gaze over to where the blackened ruins of some building lay almost hidden amongst a mass of morning glory creepers, pink and blue and purple against the pale green grass.

"There is quite a story attached to these ruins," Bill exclaimed, taking her hand to help her over the last few yards of rocky ground. The bush had encroached and what had once been a neat garden had reverted back to jungle. A fragment of wall remained standing and Fenn let her imagination wander, thinking of the hardships endured by the Missionary's wife on the difficult journey to this spot. Of the racking journey by ox-wagon, the fever and heat and wild creatures that abounded in those days. And yet, amidst all that hardship and anxiety, the woman had found time to make a garden, a home . . .

"What — what happened to the family?" Fenn felt she had to know.

Bill shrugged. "Haven't a clue! Probably came to their senses and went back to civilization."

Fenn gazed at him, a certain agitation making her frown. "You know, Bill, for someone who has made their money out of this country and the African people, you talk with such contempt."

"I didn't make money out of them, my dear Fenn, my father did."

"No, but you are not adverse to using the money for your own enjoyment, are you?"

Again that shrug. "Oh, come on, cool it! What's with you today? You're like the prickles on that thornbush over there." He gave a sly grin and attempted to circle her waist with his arm. "You pretend you're prickly but you're not really. You weren't like that at the plateau yesterday, or last night outside your verandah, before Frank, dear old watchdog that he is, called you in."

"Maybe I don't like hearing the founders of this country ridiculed," replied Fenn hotly. She turned to retrace her steps shrugging his arm away in an admonishing manner.

No more was said on the short drive to the hospital and as they approached Fenn saw Jason Kemp standing on the steps leading to the verandah, watching them as Bill parked the car. Jason's dogs, never very far from his side, barked excitedly but at a low murmur from Jason became silent.

Bill helped Fenn from her seat and glancing sideways at Jason, said, "Doctor Schweitzer himself!" He spoke in a jocular manner but the young doctor eyed him almost with hostility, thought Fenn. He transferred a frowning look upon her and said briefly, ignoring Bill's witticism, "Miss Proctor informed me of your intentions, Fenn. If you really mean it about helping, follow me."

The long ward was more crowded than Fenn had ever seen it. Beds were pushed against the walls and far doors, which were closed to the heat outside. The curtains were drawn and inside the air was heavy and warm and smelled strongly of antiseptic. Jason led them to where an African boy lay on a bed. His face was grey, his breathing harsh.

Jason turned to Fenn and said quietly, "Miss Proctor tells me you've had measles. Is that correct?" At Fenn's nod he went on, "Right, then. I want someone to sit here with this boy and call out if — and when — he wakes up. I cannot spare a nurse for this sort of thing at the moment and I really would be grateful if you would do this, Fenn."

Fenn smiled and said softly she would be only too glad to, gazing at the young boy with eyes of compassion.

Bill looked over her shoulder. "You're wasting your time," he said, bluntly. "I've seen them look like this too many times to know they seldom recover once they get that look about them."

"Maybe," Jason said. "Then, maybe not."

181

Bill looked at him oddly. "He's too far gone. Even I can see that. Why all this fuss over a kid?"

Jason did not even bother to answer, Just bent over the boy to lay a hand on his forehead, a forehead beaded with sweat. He turned to say something to the African orderly, standing attentively at the other side of the bed.

"Burying yourself in a place like this." Bill spoke again. "They don't appreciate it, you know! There must be an easier way to make a living!"

"There's always an easier way to do anything," replied Jason mildly, and now there was amusement in his voice, amusement in the grey eyes that sought and held Fenn's. "If that is what you are looking for."

But not, thought Fenn, in order to live the sort of life he'd chosen above all others . . .

She turned to a now impatient Bill. "I don't want to keep you, Bill. I'm sure you've got plenty to do. I'm going to stay a bit and help if I can. Thank's for the lift and the visit to the ruins. We'll do it again another day and perhaps explore a little further. I'll telephone Frank when I'm ready to go home and either he can come and get me or send a driver."

Bill stared at her, something like awe in his eyes. "My dear Fenn, you amaze me at times! However, if that be your wish, you know I would go to the ends of the earth to carry it out." He gave an exaggerated little bow, which also included Jason and with a nonchalant wave walked down the ward and through the door at the far end.

Aware that Jason's eyes were upon her, Fenn gave a little laugh and exclaimed, "Bill's such a fool! Sometimes more than others."

He answered, simply. "Quite!" and once again she was aware of the mockery in his voice, the mockery that so infuriated her. "It isn't his fault that his father is rich, that he has no need to work," she began hotly. "His fooling is really quite harmless."

"Is it?" His grin broadened. "Who better to know than you, my dear Fenn, as young Paynter is so fond of calling you." Even though his voice was serious his eyes were still mocking.

She opened her mouth to reply, the sudden colour deepening in her cheeks, adding sparkle to her eyes. It was one of Jason's more maddening attributes that he should be capable of goading her into losing all her dignity and descending to tossing words with him. She bit her lip and turned her attention back to the sick boy.

"Shall we get on with our work, Doctor Kemp, or would you rather have a debate on the manners, or lack of them, of certain people?"

He gave a deep chuckle. "I deserved that. I'm sorry. Put it down to the extra strain I am under just now. I think almost every village in the radius of twenty-five miles has some cases of measles, some extremely bad."

That evening she sat on the verandah of White Waters with Frank and her uncle. Selina had just brought out the tray of coffee and Fenn busied herself pouring cups for the two men. They, as usual, spoke of the farm, of the mealies ripening in the warm sun of the last few days, for, in spite of hopeful forecasts from the weather men, no more rain had fallen. "But we must have rain," Uncle Simon remarked, the tiny coffee cup looking incongruous in his large hand.

"How is that new 4,000 acre section doing, Frank?" he went on.

Frank smiled. "It's been a battle, and with a bit of luck we should reap a good three quarters of our original quota . . ."

Fenn sat in her chair, sipping the strong black brew that was her uncle's idea of coffee, her eyes gazing unseeingly at the moon-drenched garden. The afternoon's memories were still vivid in her mind; the face of the boy over whom she watched, his eyes opening at last, nervous, wondering where he was, the realization that she was his friend, that whatever he wanted she would get him. His first thought had been for water, then, sipping it, his eyes curious, only a lighter brown than his skin, he asked hesitatingly for his parents.

Fenn honestly did not know, so let him drink his fill then pushed him gently back against his pillow, promising she would endeavour to find out. Nurse Yasmin, busy at a bed at the other end of the ward, said in answer to

Fenn's question, "His mother and father are . . . " She lifted her shoulders under the white uniform in that hopeless gesture universal to the East, and, Fenn was fast discovering, Africa itself.

The nurse's dark eyes, soft with pity, gazed into Fenn's clear blue. "They reached us far too late. If only they had set out for the hospital days before they did . . . " Another shrug. "There is one consolation, if you can call it that. His baby brother is all right and the doctor seems to think they will recover quite quickly, being so young."

Fenn bit her lip, one hand going to her mouth. Suddenly she felt a rage take hold of her at the injustice of things.

"What will happen to the boy, now?" she asked. "He can't be much more than twelve or thirteen."

A shake of the dark head. "I don't know, Miss Fenn. We do have a school here, although its only for girls and Doctor Kemp intends to start one for the boys soon as he can find the time. We will teach them woodwork and mechanics, just as we teach the girls simple cookery and housework." She reached over and squeezed the slim shoulder of the girl she, and indeed, all the hospital staff, had come to know and love these last few months. "Don't worry, Miss Fenn. The doctor will think of something."

Listening to her, Fenn noted the assurance in her voice, the staunch belief that the doctor was a sort of god, that he could not fail them. She returned the nurses smile. "I'm sure you are right, Yasmin."

But, she thought desperately, what am I to say to the boy? Walking slowly back towards the bed she racked her brains for a way to pass on the news that his parents had been too far gone. That, this time, the doctor had been unable to help them . . .

But, as if in answer to her prayer, Jason suddenly appeared in the doorway and came towards her between the beds, his eyes seeking hers, almost as if he knew of her dilemma. Without a word he stood before her, noting the pale face, the full bottom lip clenched in small white teeth, the silent appeal in the blue eyes.

Paradoxically he smiled, then lowering his eyes to the boy on the bed, he said,

"Well, now, Tirimundi, you seem to have had a nice sleep. Feel like any supper yet?"

The boy looked up at him, then a smile broke through his apprehensions and he nodded eagerly. "A little, please, Doctor Bwana."

Fenn went to give Jason's instructions to Nurse Yasmin, busy once more in the ward, glad of an excuse to be away from the boy's side when Jason told him of his parents. Silently she called herself a coward, feeling Jason would despise her for this. She felt tears pricking behind her eyes and blinked rapidly, anxious in case Jason noticed and made some more of his reprimanding remarks . . .

"Fenn!" Uncle Simon's voice brought her back to the moonlit verandah. He was gazing at her with anxious eyes. "Are you all right, dear?"

She nodded, and stood, placing her cup and saucer on the small table before her. "I guess I'm a bit sleepy, uncle. I think I'll have an early night."

"You probably did too much at the hospital," her uncle told her sternly. "Don't forget you've only just recovered from a bout of fever yourself." He shook his head, frowning. "I must speak to Jason. Mustn't let you overtire yourself. Not used to the heat . . . "

Fenn smiled, bending to kiss the top of the white head on her way passed. "Nonsense! I could work at that place all day and not even notice it."

Frank, silent until now, pipe in mouth, smiling like a benevolent uncle, chimed in with, "Your uncle's right, Fenn. Don't overtire yourself. It doesn't do in this climate. Plenty of rest is what you need in this heat, at this time of the year."

Fenn wrinkled her nose at him, pausing at the door, one hand on the knob. "Like you and Uncle Simon, I suppose. I don't notice you two lying down of an afternoon."

"I do when I can," her uncle rejoined. His look sharpened. "I hear they are in the middle of an epidemic over at Mluba? I don't know that I approve of you being over there at such a time, Fenn."

"It's only measles," she told them, and thought, wryly, only! "Anyway," she went on. "Miss Proctor asked if I would be willing to assist and I said yes.

I didn't think you'd mind, Uncle Simon. Of course, if you really insist, I'll . . . "

"Knowing you modern young ladies, I don't suppose it would make a bit of difference if I did object," her uncle smiled, but there was no rancour in his voice.

Frank coughed. "I should imagine, Simon, if you really wanted Fenn to cease going to Mluba, she would. Fenn, although a 'modern young lady,' as you put it, is also very concerned about *your* health and I'm sure would do nothing impetuous to harm it."

Fenn's pretty face showed concern at this remark. "Of course, Uncle. If you really want me to stay home . . . "

Her uncle waved a hand. "I'm sure Jason will keep an eye on you, and Miss Procter's too much of a friend of mine to let you come to any harm. No, dear, you go and see what you can do. I know how short staffed they are. The Government's niggardly about the salary paid to such institutions and they can never get enough staff, not staff that will stay, anyway." He paused for a moment, considering his remark. Then went on,

"*If* the rumour should be correct, what they are going to do when Jason packs up and goes is anybody's guess. The whole place will be in a turmoil."

As Fenn hurried down the passage to her room she heard Frank's voice asking, "Do you suppose it's right, sir? Old Jason leaving us, I mean . . . "

She told herself she didn't care. While she was here she would do what she could to help these people. If, after her return to England, or even before, Jason left with Helene for more profitable climates, well, that was no affair of hers. Good luck to them both. But sleep was long in coming.

9

THE following morning she drove over to find the boy, Tirimundi, much improved and that, in fact, no new cases had arrived since the preceding day. "I think we've finally got a grip on it," Jason told Miss Procter, as she poured tea for them later that morning.

"I hope so. The ones here are not so bad. It's the poor things that are sick in their villages I worry about," she answered, ruefully.

"I thought of doing a tour of the more badly hit villages this morning," Jason said. He turned to Fenn, grey eyes summing her up. "What's your programme today, Fenn?"

"I don't know. I haven't anything important to do. Frank and my uncle will be busy most of the day in the fields."

Jason gave a quick nod. "I *was* going to ask if you would like to come with me, see at first hand the way these people live. You seem to have a sympathy for them that is rare in these days of indifference to other people's cares. And I'm not being sarcastic, in spite of what you might think." She felt the old tightening of her nerves, then, looking up into his eyes, saw that this time he meant it.

"I'd — I'd love to," she breathed, "If you think I won't be in the way!"

"As I believe I remarked once before, when you made an inane remark like that," Jason told her lightly. "You'll be the first to know if you are."

"I'll telephone your uncle to say you might be a little late," offered Miss Procter, rising.

"All right," said Jason. "Come on, then, Fenn."

After they left the hospital grounds the track became rougher and Jason's ancient car jogged and threw Fenn about until she was sure every bone in her body was bruised. He had refused the offer of the Land-Rover, saying his car knew these roads, besides which the villagers might become alarmed if they saw another, strange, vehicle, appear. The noonday sun was blazing hot. The bush seemed deserted, the animals gone to their resting places in the shade. Then as they turned a corner they saw two giraffes appear through the trees at the roadside, long necks swaying alarmingly as they broke into a sudden gallop and crossed the road only feet in front of the car. The young doctor brought the vehicle to a halt, waiting until the animals had vanished once more into the thick bush. Then he engaged gear and turning his head caught Fenn's widened eyes.

"I imagined there would be more wild animals," she told him, feeling the silence had gone on long enough.

"Did you think there would be lions and elephants roaming freely all over your uncle's garden?" he grinned, turning his attention once more to the road. "Most people seem to think that. They haven't a clue what Africa is really like."

Fenn drew a deep breath of the sun scorched, dust-laden air. Mingled with it was the smell of growing things, of syringa trees with their long yellow blossoms that grew in clusters everywhere, the fainter smell of wood smoke from a village they had passed a little while back. She thought her memories of Africa would include, beside sun baked earth and lush grass after a tropical downpour, the diversity of smells one caught when out on a drive such as this. She murmured, such a tone of contentment in her voice Jason smiled to himself slowly, "I love this country. There always seems to be such a lot happening."

"Don't you miss the bright lights and gaiety of London?"

Fenn gave a little laugh. "Everyone asks that, but really, it's only these last two years I'd lived there, since my mother . . . my parents died."

Jason removed his eyes for a brief moment to look at her, then looked back as she went on, "We lived near Bournemouth. Two years ago my father retired. My parents bought a caravan and were like a couple of children, planning tours all over Britain and the Continent. They spent that first summer touring Devon and Cornwall. Then, within a few miles of home they took a bend in the road too fast, we never really got the full story, and the caravan tipped over, dragging the car with it. They were both . . . "

"Please!" Jason's voice was deep, very gentle. "I shouldn't have asked . . . "

"No, I can talk about it now, although it took a long time. Well, I sold the house at Bournemouth and went to work in London. I liked it at first, the noise and bustle and, oh, everything. And, I suppose, the freedom. Then, a little while ago came Uncle Simon's letter. He'd asked me before to come and live with him, my mother was his younger sister, and this time I accepted." She drew a deep breath and turned her lovely head to face him. "I have to see over the next hill, don't you?"

He nodded. "I like seeing new places, doing new things, and generally I make up my mind in a hurry. Like coming out here. One minute it seemed Uncle Simon's letter was waiting for me, the next minute I was on the plane."

There was silence while she gazed at the landscape with unseeing eyes. Then she said, in so low a voice he could hardly hear her. "That's the first time

I've spoken about my parents' death except to Uncle Simon."

"They say it's always easier to talk to strangers than to friends." He moved his hand from the wheel and laid it for an instant on her knee. The touch of his fingers burned through the material of her jeans and onto her skin. She had never before been so aware of him. She felt foolish tears prick the back of her eyes and turned her head away so he would not notice.

At the same time Jason changed gears to negotiate a particularly bad stretch of track. There was a rustling of grass and across the road strolled a wart-hog and litter of six piglets. The mother hesitated, snorted at the front wheel of the car as Jason slowed almost to a standstill. Then she continued on her way, followed by her squealing brood. It was just what Fenn needed to shake her from her sudden fit of depression, and she laughed aloud as Jason murmured, his eyes on the waggling behind of the forbidding mother. "Hideous she might be, but to her family she's no doubt a queen."

They drove over a rise and there was the first village in front of them. There was a cluster of beehive-shaped huts. A few scraggy chickens pecked at the hard ground and a skinny dog lolled against the wall of a hut, scratching itself. Groups of women appeared at the sound of the car, and stood gazing silently at them, children hanging onto their mother's skirts, gazing at Fenn with huge eyes. Near a thick clump of banana trees at the edge of the village Jason stopped the car and helped Fenn from it.

"Do you want to come in with me, or would you prefer to stay under the shade of the Indaba tree and wait? I warn you, it'll be a lot cooler under the tree. The huts have little ventilation."

"I'll stay outside, thanks, Jason." She gazed at him, narrowing her eyes against the brightness of the sun. "And what on earth is an 'Indaba' tree?"

"Indaba means a meeting, a big talk. Everything of importance to the village is discussed under this tree," looking upwards into its dark foliage under which they stood. "Men only, of course." His mouth twisted in a wry smile. "Here, a woman's opinion counts as nothing, being mere chattels for the desires of their men."

He grinned down at her, teasing, testing her reaction, and she wrinkled her nose in reply and his grin widened. Before he disappeared into the interior of the dark huts, the women brought small gourds of native beer, both hands holding the gourds politely at arm's length. Fenn's drink had hundreds of tiny little sugar ants floating on the creamy froth, but for politeness sake she drank it as and when Jason did. Afterwards she amused herself by watching the children and, later on, as the sun began to sink swiftly behind the far hills, the women as they went about their preparations for their evening meal.

She was surprised when Jason hurried over to say they had better hurry if they wanted to arrive back before dark. The time had simply flown!

"The clouds are building up," he said, casting a wary eye to the range of hills where huge banks of purple clouds where beginning to pile up, partly with the coming of night, partly heralding a storm. As they began their journey back, Fenn could see, far away to the north, from the spreading clouds, a thin line was spilling, a little dark column . . .

It was raining far away. Even as she watched the line thickened.

As they drove away, the children running after them, calling shrill goodbyes, Jason said, at her enquiry as to how his patients were, "We're fortunate its no worse, really. Some of those cases could have proved fatal."

"Why didn't they come down to Mluba Hill?"

"They have such faith in their own witchdoctors, and very little in us. In fact, they have very little confidence in us at all."

Fenn smiled. "We haven't been around as long as the witchdoctors."

"Could be something in that." After a moment's silence he went on, eyeing the darkening sky with trepidation. "Rain about two miles away. Going to be heavy, too."

"Look, its coming closer," Fenn breathed, as, fascinated, she watched the dark streak broaden and approach, the lightning flashing now and thunder deep growls overhead. Zig-zag, the lightning darted overhead and the hills were lost completely in the thunder clouds. Then the rain came. Icy-cold, it bounced high off the sun-baked earth, and within moments they were soaked.

Jason bent forward, trying to see through the lashing rain and there was a sudden jolt, a revving of the engine and the car came to a halt.

Cursing softly under his breath, he said, "Sit still while I see what's the matter."

Fenn sat and shivered, arms clasped tightly across her breast in an effort to keep warm. The ancient car gave little shelter and after what seemed an age Jason's head appeared, wet and shiny and looking for all the world like a seal after a swim!

Irreverently she giggled and he said, "Save the laughing till later. You'll have to get out."

"Why?"

"The engine's stopped in case you didn't notice."

"You mean it won't go at all?"

"That's what I mean." He sounded grim and Fenn slid hastily from the wet seat onto the still wetter ground. "What are we going to do now?" she asked.

"Walk." She saw him look round at the dripping foliage, at the rapidly forming pools of rain water on the corrugated road. "Come on," he went on. "Let's see if there's some way through this jungle."

Fenn stumbled through the wet grass, following Jason's back. Apart from glancing around every few minutes to reassure himself she was still there, he said nothing, concentrating on finding a way through the thick bush. "Can't we go back to the village?" she asked wearily.

"The river's between us and the village now," he answered. "After this, it will be in full spate. Dare not try to cross it now." He turned for a brief moment, grinning at her in a reassuring manner. "I have an idea the route we are following is a short cut, if the rain and the dark setting in so early hasn't put me off. Hope so, anyway."

But in spite of his words it was

soon obvious that they were utterly and hopelessly lost and to make matters worse they came across another river which would have to be crossed if they weren't to spend the night in the rain-soaked bush. They stood on its banks, watching with sinking hearts as it swept along, a wide stretch of muddy, tumbling water that terrified Fenn. As Jason walked up and down, searching for a place to cross, cursing at what was usually a dry river bed, Fenn sat on a stump of fallen tree, feeling utterly wretched and knowing that without her to worry about Jason would have been a lot better off.

Finally he came back to where she sat and told her that about a hundred yards along the bank a huge tree had been uprooted and had lodged against a tall upright rock which divided the river into two streams. His plan was to walk along the tree which would take them almost to the other side and from there they could wade in comparative safety.

She wondered a little at his use of the word, 'comparative,' but said nothing and followed him to where the old tree lay on its side, tangled roots thrust into the air. Jason climbed on first and then hauled her up. The bark was rough, even through the soaked material of her jeans she could feel it, grazing her knees and hands. Frightened as she was she had no alternative but to follow him, trying not to look down. It was difficult to keep her balance and the sound of the rushing muddy water below mesmerized her, making her want to look down which she knew would be fatal.

One foot at a time she advanced. As they began their perilous journey Jason had given her his hand to steady her and to this she clung tight. The tree came to an end about three quarters of the way across and they had to jump down and wade the rest of the way. The water pulled and tugged, urging them to go with it but Jason's grip was strong and when finally he dragged her up the red muddy bank she was almost exhausted.

She sat on the bank, taking deep breaths while, for the first time, he appeared concerned and said, "Are you all right? We'd better find somewhere to rest. You can't go on like this."

Alarm flickered inside her, briefly, then

looking up into the clear grey eyes and worried frown, she laughed shakily and exclaimed, "That's the best idea you've had yet. I don't think I could take any more. Your pioneer women must have been really something."

He said something that sounded like "Humph . . . " and began to stride at a brisk pace along the river bank, Fenn trying in vain to keep up with his long strides. At last, unable to go another step, she came to a halt, sinking onto the trunk of a fallen tree, her head falling forward, dark hair in a bedraggled mess over her face.

"Jason!" she called, feeling awful, feeling as though her last moment had come. Surely now he would be at his sarcastic worst?

He stopped and looked back. "Fenn, we can't stop now . . . " Then realizing she must have come to the end of her tether, he retraced his steps. His voice, as he knelt beside her, was strangely gentle. "What is it, my dear?" he asked.

Lifting her head she tried to push the wet hair from her eyes, only to have him say, "No, don't try . . . "

A gentle hand brushed the hair from her face. His hand felt chilled and icy and she thought she detected a shiver run through him as he touched her. "You're exhausted," he murmured. "I'll have to carry you."

She tried to protest, knowing he must feel almost as tired as she, knowing the rough terrain over which they must still travel. But in spite of her protests he bent and lifted her in his arms. His face was only inches from Fenn's and he smiled as he murmured, "Maybe the ancient gods that protect the people hereabouts will feel sorry for us and give us shelter for the night." He carried her easily, effortlessly, like a child.

She lay perfectly still. Forgotten the chilly wetness. Forgotten the fact that they might be miles from anywhere faintly resembling a shelter. His arms were around her, his heart beating against hers. That, to Fenn, was the most important thing in life.

She seemed to drift into a sort of euphoria, coming to earth with a start as he suddenly exclaimed. "There's something over there! Could be a disused rangers hut. I forgot there were still a number of these around, although not used as much as they once were."

"Oh, I do hope so," she murmured. "You may be absolutely worn out after carrying me all this way."

Fractionally his arms tightened. "A mere ten minutes, Fenn. That's all it's been."

"Seems like a lifetime," she murmured, feeling slightly delirious, and he looked sharply down at her, saying, "What? I didn't get that!"

"Nothing. Look, I'm sure it's a hut. Let's hope it's nice and dry and doesn't leak."

He grinned ruefully. "There isn't much that will keep out the sort of rain we've just had, least of all an old hut like this."

"Don't be such a pessimist," she told him, surprised at her own tartness. "It isn't done to look a gift horse in the face and it a roof over our heads. What more can one ask?"

He looked down at her with raised eyebrows and replied, humbly, "Yes, ma'am. If you say so, ma'am."

Then laughing together they entered the dark hut, Jason pushing the creaking door open with ease. Spider webs hung from the ceiling and the tiny square windows were so engrimed with dirt and dust they were practically useless. But, as Fenn had hoped, it *was* dry, built as it was beside the protection of a thick clump of trees and surrounded with bushes.

"This will do nicely," she said, gazing around her.

Jason laughed. "I suppose I should be thankful I'm stuck here with you and not Helene. I can't for the life of me imagine her saying such a thing."

Ignoring the sudden shaft of pain the remark caused her, for even to be reminded of Helene Starr at such a time was tormenting, she went on, gaily, "Look, there's even a fireplace of sorts and over there some logs of wood." She shivered suddenly, uncontrollably.

Jason, noticing this, answered, "Yes, and looking at you I think we'd better waste no time in getting a fire lit."

"This is better," he reflected some time later. "Can't take you back to your uncle with pneumonia, can we?"

Fenn thought that this might still happen. Her thin shirt and pants were plastered to her body, her hair matted on her cheeks and forehead and raindrops trickled down her neck in a most disagreeable way. She could not, try as she might, stop shivering, and was anxious that Jason would not notice and worry even more. I bet he doesn't ask me to go on a trip with him again in a hurry, she thought, ruefully. But how extremely kind he had turned out to be! Now, seeing her shivering he came over to where she sat by the first flickering flames of the fire and stared down at her thoughtfully.

"Are you very cold?" he asked.

Dumbly she nodded, not trusting her voice to speak, she was shaking so much. Without a word he began to divest himself of his jacket and then his shirt, saying as she watched with widening eyes, "My shirt is fairly dry, dryer than my jacket, anyway. It'll be better than nothing."

Coming over to her he wrapped it around her, tying the arms in front across her chest. She let him, sitting like a child while he fussed over her, finally saying, "There, how's that?"

Suddenly there came a sound that froze her blood, making her catch her breath in terror. It was a long resonant, cavernous roar followed by a series of short coughs. It sounded infinitely menacing and frighteningly near.

"The lion is quite a way off," said Jason, watching her. "You needn't be afraid." Fenn was glad he'd said that, although she didn't completely believe him. About not being afraid, anyway.

The logs had caught alight by now, casting a cheerful glow across the dark room. Outside the storm was nearly over, the wind had died down and the only sound was the steady drip drip of the rain from the roof. The sky was completely black by now and for a moment Fenn thought of Uncle Simon, of how worried he would be. But of course he would know she was with Jason and perhaps not worry so much. Miss Procter would have phoned . . .

"Warmer now?" Jason asked, coming

to squat beside her at the fire. Fenn nodded, still not trusting herself to speak, for in spite of the gradual heat of the fire she still shivered.

He gazed at her in silence for a long moment, then said, firmly, "Don't lie. You know you're not." Without another word he placed an arm round her, drawing her close to him, then looking down at her, grey eyes smiling into blue, he kissed her forehead lightly, as one would a child.

"Try to sleep," he murmured. "We can't make a move until morning."

Acutely conscious of each other, for she felt the tension in him as well, sleep refused to come and after a while Jason began talking.

He spoke of his early life in London, of his training, and Fenn pictured the eager young doctor and his never-ending questions. "I wasn't terribly popular with the powers-that-be," he grinned, "I asked too many awkward questions. I think that's why they decided to pack me off to a way-out place like Mluba Hill. Couldn't do *too* much damage there, they figured . . . "

She woke during the night. His arms were still round her, in fact he was sitting up, propped against one wall of the hut, as close to the smouldering fire as he could get, and she lay across his chest, her own arms round his waist, face pressed into his chest. She looked up quickly, to see his eyes were still closed, his breathing steady and deep. It did not strike her as being at all peculiar to be in his arms. It seemed as natural as it was sensible, not to waste their mutual warmth.

It was light when she awoke next. The first pale sun of morning filtered through the trees and a soft glow of apricot lit up the eastern sky. Jason was still holding her, awake and smiling down at her as she opened her eyes and yawned widely. The dark shadows of his chin made him look faintly sinister. "You had a nice sleep," he remarked.

Fenn blinked. "Did you manage to get any?"

"A bit." He unfolded his arms from her and stood up, stretching like a cat. Against the morning light he looked tall and bronzed and very virile. "The rain's stopped," he said. "We'd better make a move."

This morning, with the land almost dry and steaming from the sun, the going was much easier, and although she was hungry, Fenn found it not too exhausting. They stumbled upon a village where the Chief knew Jason and within an hour or so an orderly from the hospital had arrived, driving Miss Procter's car. But before returning to Mluba Hill Jason insisted upon taking Fenn to White Waters.

"Your uncle will be at his wits' end, wondering what's become of you," he said. They found Uncle Simon at breakfast. He explained, "We weren't really worried. Miss Procter telephoned to explain that Jason hadn't returned so we just assumed you'd both taken shelter somewhere. I knew you would be perfectly safe with Jason."

Fenn grinned wearily. "Does that mean that my reputation couldn't possibly he in jeopardy as long as I was with Jason?"

"Certainly! He's too well known and respected, both by the Africans and the farmers, for titbits of gossip to do him any harm. Now, if you had gone off with Bill, that would have been a different matter."

"Really!" Fenn looked amused. "Is Bill, then, such a roué?"

"Of course not. Let's just say I was a lot more comfortable thinking of you with Jason than with Bill Paynter."

All the same Fenn was relieved that Jason had been her companion in the storm, although Bill had never actually done anything to make her feel uncomfortable, in spite of the stolen kisses and tomfoolery. Bill was really quite harmless, in spite of his air of devil-may-care man about town.

Of Helene's reaction she was left in no doubt at all. Fenn had been gathering flowers in the garden, tall shaggy petalled dahlias, at their glamorous best in this summer season, and was arranging them in vases on a kitchen table Ellias had cleared for her, when Selina came to tell her the Madam Helene had called. Helene wore dark glasses and a lemon dress that showed off her tiny waist and plenty of bosom. It was while they were drinking coffee on the verandah that

Helene launched her attack.

"I hear you've taken to visiting Doctor Kemp and the hospital?"

The dark girl lifted the cup to her lips, velvet brown eyes studying Fenn over the rim. "I also hear you were — um — marooned with him last night in the storm. Didn't get home until this morning."

"That's right," replied Fenn, calmly. She brushed a crumb from her lap, smiling at Helene serenely.

"If I were you I'd be rather more careful of my reputation," went on Helene, smoothly. "You're new here and possibly you don't realize there are things you could get away with in England that you cannot here. I'm telling you this for your own good . . . "

"And because you want Jason Kemp for yourself," thought Fenn, wryly.

"I'm sure neither you or your uncle want people talking," Helene added, still in that smooth as cream voice.

"And I'm sure there's nothing *you'd* like better," thought Fenn, so unperturbed that she surprised herself.

"Of course, Jason is always the

gentleman, under any circumstances," went on the dark girl. "But unfortunately not everyone's morals are as high." She paused meaningfully. It was a deliberately venomous remark and one that called for some sort of answer from Fenn. Luckily she was saved by Uncle Simon's appearance in the open french doors that led from the lounge.

"Ah, Helene! Always does these old eyes good to see you. How are you these days, and how is that old rogue of a grandfather of yours? Never comes to see me these days."

Helene smiled, one of her special smiles reserved for the opposite sex, Fenn was amused to notice. "Grandfather is very fit, Mr Chase. He doesn't like the heat and prefers to stay quietly indoors during these summer months."

Simon Chase lowered himself with a sigh into one of the cane lounging chairs. "Can't say I blame him. The sun can be the very devil at times. Hear about my niece's little adventure last night, eh? Good job she was with Jason. Would have been on pins if it'd been with anyone else."

His eyes twinkled as they rested fondly on Fenn. There was silence while they sipped their coffee, watching one of the garden boys who, with a long-handled brush, was busy sweeping up the mass of blue that was all that remained of the jacaranda.

The old man sighed. "The jacaranda season lasts such a short time. I'm always sorry to see it pass."

"Personally, I can't wait for Christmas and to get away to civilization once more," Helene remarked. "These next two months can't go fast enough for me."

"Are you leaving us, then, Helene?" asked Fenn quietly, conversationally.

Helene's dark eyes regarded her thoughtfully. Her full red lips narrowed into a peevish line. "Yes, and Jason Kemp will be going with me. But you knew that, of course, that Jason and I were going to be married."

Uncle Simon raised bushy white eyebrows. "Really! Can't say I'm surprised. I don't suppose anyone in the valley will be, although we'll be sorry to see him — you both," he amended hastily, "go."

After Helene had gone, a cloud of dust between the now almost bare jacarandas the only sign of her passing, Fenn went to her room to lie down, one hand shielding her eyes from the brightness of the world outside her bedroom window. She still felt extremely shaken from her night's experience and Helene's visit had not helped one bit.

Never before had she felt about a man as she now so suddenly and irritably felt about the young doctor from Mluba Hill. Indeed, she felt so miserable that she caught herself thinking, "If this is falling in love then I can well do without it." But she knew she could not do without it and no amount of self-mockery about foolish passions that would pass could make her feel any better.

10

SOME weeks had passed and Fenn had settled down into the routine of helping Ellias with the meals and Daisy about the house. Several times she had gone over to see Miss Procter, but she had not seen Jason again nor was she sure that she wanted to. Helene's reaction to their little escapade had bothered her more than she liked to admit, even to herself.

Angie had arrived that morning, her hair standing out in a golden aureole around her head as it did when she was particularly excited and had ridden through the dew-decked veldt at full gallop.

"Wonderful news, Fenn. Daddy's agreed to give a braaivelies and dance on Christmas day, and it's going to be a huge affair. He says he's never really welcomed you to the valley and that there must be dozens of other people you haven't yet met." She hugged Fenn, eyes shining. "Isn't it wonderful?"

Fenn laughed at her enthusiasm. "Wonderful," she agreed. "But, pardon my ignorance, what is a braaivelies?"

"It's like a bar-b-que, African style. We usually have it by the swimming pool and the young people wear bikinis or whatever you like to wear. The grown-ups sit in groups of garden chairs and drink and talk and the men do the cooking." Seeing Fenn's look, she went on, "Over an open fire, silly. Daddy's got a super one, on wheels, heated by gas, and we can wheel it anywhere, for someone always complains of smoke in their eyes."

"Hmmm," Fenn commented. "It does sound fun. What if it rains?"

Angie shrugged. "Who cares? We usually jump into the pool then while the others run inside. We can always wheel the fire under shelter somewhere and go on with the cooking. Rain's never spoiled a party yet, so, don't let that worry you."

Christmas day was now only a week away and Angie chattered on about a new dress and how the shop in the village would have to suffice for their needs. "I haven't really anything suitable," she said. "Would you come with me and help me choose something, Fenn?"

"I thought you said you usually wore a bikini?" Fenn remarked.

The other girl shrugged. "Oh, I've plenty of those, but Frank always glares at me so much when I appear in one that this year I decided I'll be a lady, see how that grabs him." She smiled mischievously at Fenn, then, almost in the same breath, looked gloomy, adding, "Not that he ever notices me, anyway, whatever I wear."

"Do you really want him to, Angie?" Fenn, used by now to the mercurial changes of the other girl, was nevertheless surprised at the despondent tone in her voice.

Angie seemed to give herself a mental shrug, drew herself up to her full five feet two and smiled. "Of course not! Who cares, anyway, what Frank Telfer thinks or doesn't think. Certainly not little Angie."

That afternoon Fenn found herself driving her uncle's car into the village and parking it under the shade of the huge flamboyant near the post office. Groups of picanins appeared as from no-where and stood about, giggling and whispering as the two girls climbed out and disappeared into the shop of 'Bibi's Boutique', as it so grandly proclaimed itself in gold letters over the door.

"Angie! How very nice to see you. Why don't you come and visit me more often?" Angie embraced an elderly woman who, at sight of them, had appeared from the dusty back regions of the shop and who now held Angie at arms length, gazing at her delightedly. "My," she went on, "how you've grown. And this must be your friend from overseas, Simon's niece. How do you do, my dear! I've heard all about you."

"I'm well, thank you," Fenn replied, wondering what exactly this woman had heard and from whom."

"But you want a new dress, dear, don't you? Let's see what we can find to suit you." She ran her hands along the racks. "Nothing too sophisticated, not for Angie Pendleton. How about this one?"

Fenn was surprised at the quality of

222

the clothes, the gown in particular that the woman was now showing Angie. It was a green and blue see-through material, with a long skirt and separate halter-neck top. The neckline plunged way down and Fenn could not suppress a grin, thinking of Frank's comments on such a gown. It had matching hot pants underneath, for decency's sake, Fenn supposed, and gaped when she heard Angie cry, "Fabulous! The very thing. I must have it, Bibi."

No question of money, no 'How much is it?' thought Fenn. How lucky to be the daughter of a wealthy farmer in this valley! She turned away, fingering the other gowns upon the rack, then turned back to see Angie emerge from the fitting cubicle wearing the new creation.

It fitted her as if it had been specially made for her and she could not help admiring herself in the long mirror, saying over her shoulder to Fenn, "*Don't* you think it's fabulous, Fenn? Won't the others be green with envy when they see me in *this* outfit."

Bibi caught Fenn's eye, pursing her lips. "Don't you think it's nice, Miss

Adams? I think it brings out the colour of her hair just wonderfully, all that green and blue, and at night, especially if there's a full moon, well . . . " Her smile broadened. "What young man could resist her."

"I think she looks very nice," Fenn agreed hastily, seeing that some comment was expected of her. "And, as you say, what young man could resist her."

The dress was packed tenderly in tissue paper and laid in a flat box, grand with its 'Bibi's Boutique' printed across it, albeit rather dusty as though it had lain in the shop a long time.

As they made to leave the shop Angie looked at Fenn and began, somewhat hesitantly, "What about you, Fenn? Do you have something suitable to wear or would you like me to . . . ?"

Fenn smiled, shaking her head. "No, love, I've got plenty of things that would be suitable. Some of them I haven't had a chance to wear yet. This, I can see, is going to be quite an occasion."

"Because, you see," Angie went on. "Helene always manages to be the most glamorous woman there and I thought this time we'd try and rival her."

Thinking of the see-through gown Angie had just purchased, the glorious shades of blues and greens merging one into the other, Fenn said they might very well do that this year. Angie's long slim legs could be glimpsed through quite clearly, the golden sun-tan enhanced by the sheer material. The low neckline and bare midriff also showed to advantage the bronzed skin.

The next few days passed by swiftly and Fenn awoke on Christmas day. Sunlight fell across the lime green coverlet and she reflected that this was high summer in Africa, and oh, so different to the last Christmas she had spent in London. Birds were calling from the trees in clear vibrant notes and a creeper tapped its new leaves against the windowsill.

Her uncle and Frank were already at breakfast and as she bent to kiss them both, wishing them a Merry Christmas, her uncle squeezed her hand and said, "And to you, my dear," and Frank smiled at her and said, "Have your breakfast then look under the tree by the fireplace. You might find something of interest there."

She tucked in with gusto at the sizzling bacon and golden fried eggs brought to her by Daisy together with grilled tomatoes and kidneys. The kitten, Imp, now very grown up and therefore much more dignified, strolled over and rubbed himself against her legs beneath the table, his purring loud in the peaceful room. Surreptitiously she slipped it a tiny piece of bacon from her plate and smiled as it ate with contentment, again rubbing its glossy black head against her when the bacon was gone.

"I still haven't got over the shock of waking to find sunshine and flowers instead of snow and rain," she smiled. "Especially on Christmas day."

Much later, when the presents had been handed out, a new pipe for Frank, a volume of poems for her uncle which, surprisingly, she found he very much enjoyed, she opened her own, crying aloud with delight at the huge bottle of perfume from Frank, who grinned sheepishly and murmured, "Never could think of anything original, sorry."

"It's gorgeous, Frank. I love perfume." Not to worry that it wasn't what she herself would have chosen. The thought was there and that was all that mattered, really. Her uncle's gift was a cardigan in soft lambs wool, "Had it knitted specially for you," he said, smiling.

Her presents to the two maids and Ellias, the cook, were received with wide eyes and solemn bowing of heads, hands clasped before them in deep gratitude. Fenn felt quite shaken that anyone could feel so grateful and show it so plainly. Her thoughts turned to the hospital and after a brief service in the tiny church in the valley that, that morning was filled to overflowing with farmers and their families, she asked Uncle Simon if he would mind if she visited the hospital before lunch.

Driving the Land-rover across the velt Fenn felt a sense of wellbeing never before equalled. A cool breeze blew, ruffling her dark hair, tendrils of it blowing across her lips and cheeks. The breeze tempered the already humid heat considerably and as she drove she found, to her astonishment, that she sang snatches from a recent pop song. "Idiot!" she told herself.

"So what if it's Christmas and you *are* going to see Miss Procter! No need to make a big thing of it!"

The hospital grounds were crowded with visiting families. Groups of women sat with children on the bright green grass, their menfolk roaming about, laughing, talking to all and sundry. The nurse, Yasmin, spied Fenn as she alighted from the landrover and, smiling, strode over to meet her. "Merry Christmas, Miss Fenn," she called. "I'm so glad you came to visit us. The doctor needs help with his costume and Miss Procter drove over to visit some friends early this morning and hasn't yet returned."

Fenn returned her smile, following her into the deep shade of the verandah. "What costume, Yasmin? Are they putting on a charade, or something?"

Yasmin frowned at the use of the word 'charade', not knowing exactly what it meant, and went on, "Well, I don't know what that is, but every Christmas the good doctor acts as Santa Claus to the children. He puts on a red outfit Miss Procter always hides away for the rest of the year and takes round presents." She giggled suddenly, picturing Jason as he struggled with the heavy red outfit endeavouring to stuff the front with a pillow and getting all snarled up in the process.

"And you want me to help him dress?" smiled Fenn, wondering how Jason would receive her presence at such a time, for she had not seen him since their parting on the verandah at White Waters on the morning after their 'escapade', as Helene so delightfully put it.

"If you would, Miss Fenn ... " Already they were entering the large airy lounge where, at one end, Fenn caught sight of Jason endeavouring to fasten a brilliant red suit, trimmed with white, about his slim middle.

She smiled widely. Not so slim now, with a pillow stuffed inside, making him bulge in all the wrong places. He turned, hearing their voices, and even had the grace to blush, widening Fenn's smile even more.

"Oh!" he said, "Ummmnn — just in time, Fenn. Perhaps you could manage to fasten me up. Miss Procter usually is here to do the necessary but today she chooses this time to be visiting. Annoying woman . . . "

Fenn came forward, managing to hide her smile, assuming a straight face as she neared him. Yasmin took one look at her superior's rather disgruntled countenance and disappeared once more through the door, back to the crowds of happy people outside.

Without a word she fastened the wide belt about the protuberant middle, trying not to catch the young doctor's eye, trying to be very businesslike and brisk about the whole process. But finally she could hold her mirth in no longer and gazing up at him, seeing, especially, the long white beard and curling moustache, collapsed in laughter on to a leather chair nearby.

"Really!" he spluttered, gazing down at her with indignation. Then he, too, saw the funny side and joined with Fenn in laughter.

Finally she said, wiping her eyes with a scrap of white handkerchief, "I shouldn't really be laughing at you. I'm dreadfully sorry. It's only that you looked so — so . . . " And she was off again, laughing until her sides ached.

He frowned, endeavouring to look stern. "All right, that's enough, Fenn. Shall we go out and give the children their gifts? If you manage to control your merriment you could help me."

Immediately she was full of self-remorse. "Of course, Jason. I'd love to. What you must think of me, laughing like that! I wasn't laughing at *you*, you must believe me."

He gave her a tight smile. "Weren't you? Never mind, whatever you were laughing at did you good." He stopped for a brief moment, gazing down at her, eyes twinkling above the absurd moustache. "It's made your eyes shine, your cheeks glow. I can't remember when I last saw you looking so sweet."

"Shouldn't we . . . " she said, hastily, quickening her step, "shouldn't we be hurrying to give these to the children? Won't they be getting impatient?"

Fenn stood and watched as Jason walked slowly amongst them, handing parcels to all. Some, smaller ones, clung to their mother's skirts, peeping in scared fashion at the tall red figure, but finally they came out and took the offered parcel with tiny black hands. Afterwards, when the sack Jason had flung over one shoulder was empty, he scattered handfuls of paper-wrapped sweets and in the following scramble escaped to where Fenn stood, smiling.

"Phew," he muttered. "That was quite an ordeal! This outfit's just about killing me, it's so hot. How about helping me out of it and then we'll have a drink."

"All right, Jason. You did a wonderful job. The children loved it."

"Hmmmn, it's a worth while job, anyway, although thank God it's only once a year." He gave a wry smile, leading the way into the cool lounge. "You don't know the half of it, though. I still have to help serve the Christmas dinner! Tradition, and all that jazz."

"This is where a wife would come in handy," Fenn began, then could have bitten her tongue, realizing what she had said. Somehow, she could not visualize Helene in the role of good Samaritan, helping the children on Christmas day.

Much more likely to be off at some party, enjoying herself.

Helene's voice came back, echoing in the quiet room like a threat to the peace and tranquillity of this happy day . . . "Of course, and Jason will be coming with me . . . You knew, of course, that we were going to be married?"

Jason was busy running fingers through the longish dark hair that would insist in falling over his forehead, now that the red cowl was removed. Beads of perspiration dotted his forehead and Fenn longed to wipe it gently away, thinking how hot he must be under all that white hair fixed to his face. For, as he explained, it was no use removing it yet, not until his duties as Santa Claus were finished, and that would not be until late afternoon, when Christmas dinner was over. They sat and sipped long cool drinks of lemon juice, soda water and ice, watching the antics of a rather large elderly lady dressed in a bright red cotton sarong type outfit, dance and jig her way about the clearing below them. Finally Jason himself was called down to the clearing while the lady told of her appreciation in song and dance before him, making Fenn laugh as she sidled up to Jason, twisting and turning as expertly as any exotic dancer in a strip club in London. Fenn called down to him, gaily, "She seems to fancy you, Jason. You've really made a conquest there."

Later they talked of the barbeque to be held at the Pendleton's farm that evening. "Are you coming, Jason?" Fenn enquired. "Angie's so excited you would think she'd never been to one before."

"Sweet child," murmured Jason, absently, watching as Miss Procter's battered car drew up and parked beneath the shaded trees below them. "Never really grew up, though."

Fenn frowned. "Who, Angie? I don't know why everyone says that about her. To me she's really a perfectly normal young woman, a bit giddy, but a woman, nevertheless."

Jason gave her an indulgent smile and the subject was forgotten as Miss Procter came into the room, full of news about her visit.

Before leaving Mluba Hill Fenn managed to see Jessica, who still worked there as housemaid until other preparations were made for her and baby Fenn. To the baby Fenn gave a few cotton dresses she had managed to make, by hand but which were nevertheless quite nice, and to Jessica herself an envelope with a gift of money, for Fenn knew that this would be more welcome to the African girl than anything else. The girl curtsied and held the envelope to her breast, gazing at Fenn with eyes full of gratitude. Before leaving Fenn also hunted out Tirimundi, the young boy she had helped to look after when he had been so sick. She'd asked her uncle's advice as to what to give him and Simon had thought a money gift would be in keeping, for the boy had little now he was alone.

Her actions were not lost on Jason for he said, smiling in the way that always notched her temperature up a couple of degrees, "You don't know how much I appreciate that, Fenn. I only wish we had a sprig of good old mistletoe to celebrate in the usual way."

Miss Procter cut in briskly, "Don't tell me, Jason, you need an excuse like a sprig of mistletoe to kiss Fenn?" She grinned, adding impishly, "Go ahead, I won't breathe a word of it. Least of all to Helene."

Fenn had no time to answer before his lips clamped down on her own. But where Bill's kisses had left her cold now she found her senses slipping away and she was relaxing in his arms, and suddenly he was kissing her with a strength and fury that frightened her. Taking a deep breath, reminding herself who *she* was and who *he* was, she lifted her face and kissed his cheek. "Thanks, Jason," she murmured, "Thanks for everything."

She was too confused to work out exactly what she meant by that 'thank you', but she knew that in those last few moments, Jason, whether he knew it or not, had irrevocably altered the relationship between them. She knew that, from now on, she could never quite meet him again on the same footing.

"Will you forgive me," she murmured, standing back and smiling at an approving Miss Procter. "I must get back to my uncle. I said I would not be long . . ."

"Of course, dear. Run along. Simon

deserves a good Christmas with you by his side." Fenn smiled and waving goodbye, drove back to White Waters with the events of the morning whirling around crazily in her mind.

11

THE party was proving a great success.

Fenn lingered in the garden enjoying the cool night air, still unable to convince herself that this was Christmas, that she stood by a swimming pool where a group of young people shouted and splashed, when really there should have been snow on the ground and the stars above her twinkling icily through a grey winter sky. Dressed in a soft drift of sun-yellow organza, her back and shoulders bare, a dazzling collar of silver sequins holding the halterneck top, she had almost to pinch herself that it was real. She felt alluring and almost seductive as the pale moon made black shadows on the grass around her. Angie had squealed with delight at sight of the dress, saying, "You old fraud! You never told me you had such a super dress to wear."

"You never asked me," Fenn smiled.

238

There were soft footsteps on the grass behind them and Frank Telfer appeared. "Hello," he grinned.

"Your uncle insisted I come to the party. Wouldn't hear of a refusal."

Angie giggled and threw her arms around his neck, much to his embarrassment. "Angie, please," he muttered, and endeavoured to push the girl away.

Angie pulled a face. "I can't remember the last time you came to one of our parties, Frank, I'm only saying Merry Christmas."

His brown eyes surveyed her smilingly. "I realize that, old girl. Just don't let's make a public spectacle of it, eh?"

Angie turned away abruptly, grabbing the arm of the young man who was with her. "Come on, Mike. Let's leave the old folks alone and go and enjoy ourselves."

Some distance away the coals still glowed and the appetizing smell of cooking meat hung in the air. "Have you eaten yet, Fenn?" Frank asked.

"No, and I'm absolutely starving."

Taking her gently by the elbow Frank guided her to the rubescent coals. "Did

239

I barge into something between you and Angie and those boys?" he enquired.

"No, of course not. Perhaps you can show me how to hold this thing in the correct fashion," Fenn laughed, holding aloft the pronged fork on which her supper dangled, a piece of steak that she eyed with some alarm.

Frank grinned and took the fork from her outstretched hand.

"I must say one has to be brought up with these things in order to be successful with them. Not that I am. Far from it. Most of the time I drop the sausage into the fire or something equally stupid."

Fenn laughed, her face glowing red in the flames of the fires, her hair outlined in a Titian glow.

After a while he rejoined her and they walked back towards the pool side, choosing a stone bench on which to sit and eat with their fingers the tasty charcoaled meat. There was plenty for both of them and Fenn said, licking her fingers, "Hmmmn, that was delicious! Why do I always imagine food eaten in the open always tastes better than that eaten at table?"

Frank chuckled. "It must be the gypsy in you," he told her. She held her hands away from her, fearful of getting, the lovely yellow dress soiled with grease. "I feel a mess, she murmured. "And this was hardly the correct outfit for such a meal."

Pulling a folded handkerchief from his pocket, Frank leaned towards her, saying, "Hold still a minute, you've got meat juice running down your chin." Feeling slightly foolish she let him dab at her chin, while he continued, eyes fixed on his delicate task, "As for the dress, I think its a knockout, and, believe me, it isn't very often I notice a woman's dress."

Fenn laughed, thinking this was probably the understatement of the year, coming from Frank. Frank never even noticed a *woman*, let alone her dress. Feeling this was the right time, she said, "Talking of dresses, what did you think of Angie's, or didn't you notice?"

Leaning back, Frank frowned, lips pursed meditatively. "Well, I must say I couldn't help but notice. The colours were lovely, but the style," and he shook his head, the frown deepening.

"Oh, come on, Frank!" Fenn laughed. "Didn't you think she looked absolutely lovely in it? Most of the other boys at the party seemed to think so, anyway, for there was no lack of partners."

"Yes, I did notice that," he conceded. Giving a last tiny dab at the offending chin, he surveyed her with so candid a look that this time she felt herself blushing. "You know, Fenn," he began, "You are an extremely pretty girl. I don't know why I didn't notice it before."

She dropped her eyes to the moon shadowed grass, one slim foot in its silver sandal toying with a little pile of fallen leaves blown there by an errant wind. "Thank you, sir," she murmured, with mock prudery. "You are too kind."

"No, seriously Fenn, you are. I'm not much good at telling girls things like that and I must confess I don't always notice, but tonight there seems to be a — how can I put it, — an enchantment about you that I've never noticed before."

Fenn wasn't too sure how to handle this side of Frank and hoped he was not going to become tiresome like most of the other young men she knew.

242

She leaned down, lifting a handful of dry leaves in her hand, then letting them drift once more to the ground. Before she could think of a suitable answer he went on, "I don't mean to be offensive, Fenn, and I did have a few drinks before leaving White Waters, perhaps that is the only way I can say what I really feel . . . "

Suddenly leaning over Fenn pressed her lips for a brief moment against his. She said, lightly, "I think I understand, Frank. It's the moon and Christmas and . . . "

There was a sudden movement behind them and they turned to see Angie, the smile on her face slowly vanishing as she stared at them through the gloom. How long had she been there? wondered Fenn. How much of their friendly lighthearted conversation had she heard?"

"Angie . . . !" she began, and to their amazement the other turned and with what sounded unmistakenly like a sob disappeared across the grass, running for the house.

Frank said, with perfect calm, "We seem to have upset her. Always was an odd child." He turned back to Fenn.

"Feel like a drink yet?"

Fenn shook her head. "No thanks, Frank. I suppose we should go and find Angie . . . see what is wrong . . . "

"Not to worry. She'll go off with one of those young boys and forget whatever it was that was bothering her in no time at all."

Fenn hesitated. Did Frank really believe that? Angie seemed most upset and Fenn felt it was really up to her to discover the reason why. But somehow the groups of young people converged on them and later, much later, when Fenn enquired of Mrs Pendleton how Angie was, for she had not made another appearance, the woman said, "She says she's got a headache. Don't worry my dear, Angie'll be all right. I've given her some tablets and made her lie down. I think she stayed in the sun too long this morning, swimming. Never will listen to reason."

Frank drove her back and said all in all it was one of the best parties he had ever attended. During the night it rained again and on the next four days and Fenn was unable to get out much.

But on the fifth day she was so weary of her own company and Sean's pleading eyes that said, "*When* are we going for a walk? Surely you don't mind a bit of rain?" she packed the large dog into the back of her uncle's car and drove over to Mluba Hill.

Wearing a souwester and long raincoat borrowed from Frank, she made an incongruous picture as she helped the dog from the car and ran through the rain towards the verandah where Miss Procter stood, smiling at her appearance. While they sat and talked over tea the rain stopped as suddenly as it had started and a watery sun poked through. "Splendid," remarked Miss Procter. "We can go for a walk. I have something to show you."

A few minutes walk from the hospital buildings took them to a quiet part of the compound where a few small buildings made up a small village.

Here Jason had installed a school, an old building but well kept and made pretty by evergreen bushes and creepers growing over it. Going inside they interrupted a lesson given by a young African girl to a small class of girls. They stood up at the visitors approach and curtsied politely, going back to their lesson when Miss Procter said, "Do go on, Elizabeth. I'm showing Miss Adams around. Some of the aspects of our hospital are new to her."

Fenn was intrigued. The young African teacher spoke in the local dialect but it was not difficult to know that she talked of personal hygiene and the care of babies, for the drawings on the blackboard that accompanied the lesson were very good.

Seeing her interest, Miss Procter smiled and murmured, "A side of Jason that you knew nothing about. He insists on these girls being taught cleanliness and the proper care of infants, for, with most of them I'm afraid, it's a very hit and miss procedure."

They walked slowly back to the house and to Fenn's surprise Miss Procter went on, "This young man, Bill. Are you going to marry him?"

"Oh, no." Fenn rejected the idea so quickly she surprised even herself. "Bill's a good sort, fun to be with, but I'm afraid he's not the marrying type. He's been very good to me, giving up his free time during the holidays to take me about, but we never were serious."

Miss Procter looked thoughtful, and Fenn gazed at her curiously.

"Why do you ask?"

"Naturally I'm interested. I'm interested to know whether you are going to stay in the valley or whether you're going to leave us. You've been a great comfort to me, Fenn, in the last few months. A great comfort to Jason, too."

"I'm grateful that you think so," trying hard not to show the elation that the older woman's words brought, the sensuous warmness that seemed to spread like an elysian blanket about her at the thought of Jason feeling grateful towards her. "I've enjoyed helping out whenever I could," she went on. "It's opened my eyes to a lot of things."

Miss Procter nodded. "Yes, a few months here and you go back to the green fields of England as though seeing them for the first time. I'm sure, too, it makes you more tolerant. I know it has me."

"I could never imagine you, of all

people, being *intolerant*." Fenn murmured, only to have the other woman shake her head, saying softly, "No, really, when I first came to Africa I expected all sorts of wonderful things. One reads of the tropical flowers and scenery, the scents and sounds and sunshine of Africa. One never reads of the more down-to-earth things, the poverty, the subjection into which their women are born and are kept for the rest of their lives. Even the educated ones have a hard time impressing their menfolk with their ability to teach or nurse or even run a decent home. That is why Doctor Kemp insists upon a school here. If we cannot do much for the older folk at least we can help enlighten the younger ones."

The older woman seemed inclined to let the subject of Bill drop after that and Fenn was only too glad to talk at length of the tiny school and the plans Jason had for the African children. She felt she could never hear enough about Jason Kemp and the future events in his life, even, she told herself bitterly, if she were not here to see it."

She drove back in the cool of the

evening when the inky shadows cast by the setting sun dappled the veldt and every rock seemed to hold some hidden and strange mystery. She imagined the insect life, the tiny creatures that lived between the sun-warmed rocks, even the snakes that, thank heavens, so far she had not seen. She wondered if they emerged at night to seek their prey and what prey it could be they caught. Other creatures, smaller than themselves? Sean, sitting inelegantly in the back of the car, quivered with excitement, nose sniffing at the window.

Eat or be eaten, that was the law of the jungle. Run or be caught, she told herself . . . What would it be like being caught by a man such as Jason . . . ? The warmth of his arms as he held her that night in the old hut came back to her so vividly that she shivered.

Fool, she reproached herself. A man like Jason Kemp is for the Helenes of this world, not the quiet dark-haired girls that, as children, had spoke only when they were spoken to and said please and thank you and pretended they didn't give a damn whether the Jasons betwixt us gave them a second glance or none at all . . .

She arrived back at White Waters to find Angie waiting for her. Fenn had not seen her since the party but had telephoned a few times and found Angie curt and uncommunicative. Now she saw a most impatient Angie who strode up and down the verandah while Frank hovered nearby with glass in hand and murmured soothingly, "Really, young lady, language such as that will get you precisely no-where around here, even if it does send your father into a tizzy at home."

Fenn pushed open the screen door leading to the verandah, Sean bounding ahead, almost knocking Angie down in his exuberant greetings. Angie turned upon Frank in a fury, her face pink with temper, her soft childish lips in a hard line. "Oh, do shut-up. I'm sick and tired of your smart alecy jokes, Frank Telfer. If you *never* speak to me again it will be too soon."

Fenn caught Frank's eye and raised her brows in enquiry. Frank shrugged his shoulders and taking another sip from his drink vanished through the open french doors to the lounge. Fenn threw the raincoat over the back of a chair, shook her dampish hair away from her face and seated herself in a chair near Angie. "Seems like I barged in at a most untimely moment. Care to tell me about it, love?"

Angie pouted, turned her back on Fenn and fingered the shiny leaves · of a pot plant that grew on a low stand by the verandah wall. "I don't know that I do," she said in a low angry voice. "You're just as bad as Frank."

Fenn raised surprised eyebrows. "I am? What are we supposed . . . ?"

Before she could finish the sentence Angie had turned on her, fists clenched tightly at her sides. "You pretend you are my friend and you act just like Helene. I thought she was the only woman I had to contend with. Now I find I have another."

"What *are* you talking about, Angie?" Fenn tried to hide the amusement in her voice, amusement that was fast turning to exasperation. "Frank and I are friends. I'm certainly no rival for his affections — or any other man's, for that matter," she added, almost defiantly.

Angie gave a derisive laugh. "No? That wasn't the impression I got the night of the party."

Fenn could not prevent herself from laughing, which only seemed to enrage the other girl still more. Fenn went on, "If you mean the scene on the lawn, you need your head examining. Frank and I were merely talking. Oh, I did kiss him, but it *was* Christmas, remember."

Angie's head was downbent. Then she looked up at Fenn. "Oh well, I suppose I have to face it sooner or later. One day Frank will bring a bride back from one of the overseas trips he does every so often, and I'll have to greet her as a new friend, as I greeted you, and invite her to tea and parties and ride across the veldt with her and . . ."

Realization came to Fenn with such a shock that she felt her heart sink in her breast. The girl was in love with the quietly spoken manager of White Waters. She probably had been for years, a schoolgirl crush that had remained, had intensified over the years and now pervaded all her thoughts and actions. This, then, was the reason for the girl's moodiness, her temperamental outbursts over the last few weeks.

Fenn said very gently, "Frank, for all his teasing, is very fond of you, Angie. Even you must recognize that."

Angie's anger was spent and she made no reply. Fenn went on, "Frank thinks the world of you, dear, but you must show him that you are no longer a child. All these tantrums in front of him won't help you one bit." Her voice was gentle and understanding and it proved Angie's undoing for she suddenly and ashamedly broke into a flood of tears. At the same moment Frank appeared once more from the direction of the lounge.

His face was a study as he gazed at the sobbing girl, then before Fenn could speak, he hurried forward and placed one arm about Angie's shoulders, drawing her down beside him on the low padded bench below the verandah wall.

When Fenn left, moving quietly away so as not to disturb them, his arms had closed round Angie and her head was buried upon his shoulder, the sound of sobbing gradually diminishing as he patted her back as one would a child.

Fenn sighed and continued on her way to her bedroom. She sat on her bed for a long time before having a shower and changing from her damp jeans and shirt. She tried to comfort herself that Angie at last had a settled future ahead of her. A future with Frank who, Fenn realized, would make the best of husbands, especially for a girl like Angie; firm, steady and tender.

And for herself? That night sleep was far away and she lay for hours staring into the darkness, wondering what fate held in store for her. She knew Uncle Simon would be only too delighted to have her stay on at White Waters. But would this be possible, knowing that Mluba Hill was so near, especially when Jason and Helene had finally married and left for pastures new . . .

The following day was hazy, the sky still heavy with clouds, seeming, like a blanket, to press the heat down upon a gasping world. Fenn did little but wander desolately about the house, Sean pottering behind her.

The black kitten was no-where to be seen but she later discovered him stretched full-length along the branch of a jacaranda tree, one paw tucked under his chest, the other dangling, eyes slitted against the heat.

That afternoon Fenn lay on her bed, endeavouring to read, having refused Frank's invitation to drive over to Msasa Ridge with him to see Angie. This was one time when Frank would prefer to go alone, she thought wryly. Her uncle had remarked that he'd asked Jason along to dinner. She must have dozed for when next she woke it was evening, a watery moon shedding a broad band of light across the foot of her bed. It was much cooler now and being used to the rapid changes of weather at this time of year Fenn guessed that more rain was not far off.

By the time she had showered and changed into a thin wool dress of burnt orange that contrasted beautifully with her dark hair and golden tanned skin, Uncle Simon and his guest were already sipping their before dinner sundowners. The two men rose at her approach and

Jason hurried forward to pull out a chair, smiling as he did so.

"What will you have to drink, Fenn?" His voice was low, melodious in the still night.

"I — I think just an orange, with lots of ice," she replied, smiling up at the young doctor. He returned her smile and went over to the corner bar that Uncle Simon had had built to one side of the verandah. Behind it, on the wall, a leopard skin was mounted and above that an African shield and crossed spears. Fenn had always thought this touch gave an air of authenticity to the general African scheme of the verandah, merging well with the cane furniture and exotic pot plants.

"Sorry you've got to do that, old man," her uncle remarked as Jason poured orange juice into a tall frosted glass, topping it with slivers of crushed ice. "Frank always does the honours for me, but tonight he's gone tearing off to Msasa Ridge for some odd reason. Looked like a young boy going on his first date."

"That's all right, sir," Jason smiled. "We've all got to take time out to relax sometimes. Dinner with a pretty girl is as good a therapy as any I know, and you must admit, Angie Pendleton is a pretty girl."

Of the night they had spent in the bush there was no mention, and although Fenn waited with a touch of apprehension in case Jason or her uncle brought up the subject, nothing was said. They had eaten dinner, young duckling garnished with orange sauce that Uncle Simon said was one of his wife's favourites and which Ellias was extremely good at making, when the telephone rang. Her uncle rose to answer it and immediately called Jason. The rain, as promised, was coming down in torrents by now and Fenn could barely make out the murmur of his voice as he spoke in the hall.

But from what little she could hear she guessed there might be trouble at the hospital. At last he put the receiver down and rejoined them in the lounge. "We've got an emergency on our hands. It seems Miss Procter is involved in it."

Fenn rose to her feet, one hand going to her throat. "Can I help, Jason? Is it bad?"

Jason's eyes went to her uncle, knocking out the ashes of his empty pipe into the fireplace and frowning. "Would you mind, sir? Fenn is always a great moral support if nothing else."

"Of course, Jason." Simon rose immediately to his feet. "I know how much Fenn admires Miss Procter and if you think she will be of any assistance to you by all means take her with you."

Fenn smiled her gratitude. She was grateful for small mercies, she told herself. Grateful for the chance to be with Jason just that little bit longer. Simon followed them to the car. "I'll get Frank to bring the car over for you, Fenn. He shouldn't be too late. Just give us a ring when you're ready."

"Don't worry, sir," Jason smiled. "I'll see that she gets back."

Staring ahead at the road Jason said, "This is awfully good of you, Fenn. You care a lot for Miss Procter, don't you?"

"I think she's an absolutely wonderful woman."

By the time they had reached the hospital the road was awash and the rain in the car's white headlights was like grey spears of rain falling from heaven.

Jason stopped the car outside the main entrance of the hospital. In the bright lamp light over the door hundreds of flying ants were battering themselves to death in a desperate flight for life. Jason got out his side and ran around to Fenn's, holding open the door and saying, "Quick, run for it. It's a real downpour."

He placed one arm around her shoulders and together they made a dash for the open doorway. Even so her hair clung wetly to her forehead and cheeks and Jason laughed, saying, "It seems every time I invite you out you get wet. I assure you it isn't my intention. It doesn't always rain in Africa. In fact, now that the jacaranda season is over we probably won't get any more after this lot."

In the emergency room doorway they met Nurse Yasmin, the Anglo-Indian girl whom Fenn had met before. She was obviously glad to see Jason and said, "Miss Procter has a nasty cut on her scalp, doctor. Come, I'll show you . . ."

Jason nodded and pushed his way

through the door, Fenn and the nurse following him. On the high bed against one wall Miss Procter lay, a bloodstained bandage wrapped roughly about her head. Her face was pale and she had a dazed expression in her eyes. As she caught sight of Jason and Fenn her face brightened and she said, "Am I glad to see you! An old woman of my age has no right to be running around in the dark and I know you'll tell me so to my face."

"I'll tell you that, and more, all in good time," agreed Jason, dryly. "But first, let's have a look at it."

Fenn stood by while the nurse removed the bandage to reveal a scalp wound that ran the length of one side of the head and left a mass of white hair oozing dark blood.

Jason sighed as he appraised the injury and then in a crisp voice directed the nurse to get scissors and other necessities. To Fenn he said, "You go over and see the cook. Get him to make you a cup of tea. I'll join you later. This will need stitches, I'm afraid."

Still Fenn hesitated. "But what happened . . . ?"

Jason took her by the shoulders and gently propelled her towards the doorway. "Do as you are told," he said. "At the moment you know as much about it as I do. I'll join you later and tell you then."

She found the cook, an elderly African who had been in the hospital's employ for years, still up and greatly disturbed by the news. He kept shaking his head and saying, over and over again, "A person isn't safe no longer, Miss Fenn. I'm telling you, they is safe no longer."

"What *are* you talking about, old man?" Fenn frowned. But the old cook was in too agitated a state to be coherent and Fenn had to be content until Jason joined her later to hear the full story.

"She heard a sound outside," said Jason grimly, accepting the cup of tea she had poured for him. "Then the dogs started barking and she thought she'd better investigate. It must have been a prowler with too much native beer inside him. Anyway, out she goes and gets knocked over the head for her pains. I'm afraid she'll have a nasty headache in the morning. Ought by rights, to go into Mwera for X-ray, but she won't hear of it."

"Why would anyone do that to Miss Procter?" asked Fenn quietly. "She's so well loved and respected around here."

He smiled, a smile that tore at her heart, so tired and weary was it, and placed one hand over hers that lay on her lap. "Heaven only knows, Fenn. Come on, let's get you back to your uncle. There's little we can do for Amy now. She just needs sleep and I've promised her you can come and visit in the morning."

"I hate letting you drive all that way back, Jason. Let me call Frank."

He shook his head. "Don't be silly. A drive in the fresh air will clear my head." The rain was still coming down strongly. In the twin beams of the headlights it seemed to Fenn as if they were marooned in time, in space, alone in a dark world where nothing else stirred. As the car came to a stop outside the lighted verandah of White Waters, Jason switched off the engine and turned to her. There was a deep silence, neither knowing what to say.

Then, almost without warning, Jason's arms were around her, pulling her tight against him. Then his voice, husky, low, whispered, "Fenn, Fenn, you're so sweet. Since that kiss on Christmas day I've been longing to kiss you again . . . "

Fenn gave him back his kiss with all the strength of her being, and at last Jason released her and, with a sigh, said, "I'm sorry. I didn't want that to happen, not quite like that, anyway."

Fenn was startled at his sudden change of manner. "Why do you say that?"

He rested a hand on the steering wheel and looked straight ahead.

"I've known for a long time I was getting more fond of you than I wanted to allow myself to. My life must run in different directions to yours. I'm sorry Fenn. Oh . . . there are a dozen things I couldn't possibly explain nor you understand. Goodnight my love."

12

FENN let herself into the house and went quietly into her bedroom, closing the door behind her. But even so her uncle heard her. There was a gentle knock at her door and at her gentle, "yes?" her uncle's voice answered. "Fenn! Are you all right, dear?"

She hurried forward to open it, to see her uncle standing there, robe over his pyjamas, and in slippers. "Yes, I'm all right, uncle. Sorry if I disturbed you. I tried to move quietly."

"You didn't disturb me. I wasn't asleep." His eyes rested on the rain and wind swept night revealed by the open curtains at the wide windows.

"It's a dreadful night! Wouldn't you like some hot milk or something?"

"I don't think so, uncle." Fenn smiled. "I'm so tired, I assure you I'll have no trouble getting to sleep tonight."

"Well, all right, dear." Still her uncle seemed hesitant to leave.

"There's a terrible storm springing up. I hope it won't frighten you." He gazed at her keenly. "How was Miss Procter, by the way? Was it every bad?"

Fenn related the whole incident, leaving out only Jason's kiss in the car. "Jason seems to think it will be satisfactory," she said. "Although it was a nasty shock for her, for all of us." Funny, she caught herself thinking, how these days she related herself with Mluba Hill. Almost as though she belonged, as did Miss Procter and Nurse Yasmin and the rest of the small staff . . .

She collected her thoughts hastily as her uncle turned to go, saying over his shoulder, "I'm glad it wasn't too bad. Old Jason has enough to cope with just now without his chief helper going sick. Goodnight, child."

In spite of her assertions of being tired, she still found she could not sleep. Jason's kiss was too near, — too *real*, for her to fall calmly asleep. Inside of an hour the wind was strong enough to sweep huge clouds over the sky and like a small hurricane tossed the jacaranda trees along the driveway with maniacal fury. Fenn lay for some time, eyes wide open, gazing out at the dark night. She was still wide awake when Uncle Simon knocked and came back into her room an hour later.

"Is the wind disturbing you, my dear?" He sounded slightly agitated and Fenn realized that probably he, too, could not sleep. "It's a bit noisy, but it doesn't bother me unduly, uncle."

Uncle Simon moved over to the window, drawing the curtains back with one hand. Fenn seldom closed them entirely. She loved to lie in her bed and watch the African moon, like a topaz ball, move across the sky amidst a blaze of stars seldom seen anywhere but in this vast and enchanting country.

"I hope it doesn't keep this up all night," he went on. "The river's fairly high now. A bit more and it'll flood."

Fenn sat up and hugged her knees. "How would that affect us?"

"There are quite a number of small villages alongside the river. A flood would affect them and their crops. Also their sheep and cattle and even goats, although these creatures generally can look after themselves. They depend such a lot on their other cattle, however."

Fenn frowned. "How awful! I hope it stops soon, then."

Her uncle shook his white head. "I don't think it will. Not for hours. These are all the signs of a good old tropical downpour. Anyway," one hand drawing the curtains once more over the wretched sight outside, and turning to smile at Fenn. "Try and get some sleep, as will I. I'll only get a telling off from Frank if I show signs of tiredness in the morning." With one last smile he was gone, closing the door silently behind him.

Fenn woke for a short time at first light. The wind had dropped. The sky was the colour of gunmetal, and the air in her room was icy. For the first time since her arrival at White Waters she found herself getting out the white wool slack suit with its emerald green sweater, roll necked and extremely cosy. At breakfast both her uncle and Frank looked worried.

"As I said, the river *has* risen," Uncle Simon told her as she joined them at the table. "There was a report over the radio that one of the bigger islands was flooded and the people living there barely managed to get away in time."

"Any news of Miss Procter?" Frank asked. Uncle Simon shook his head. "Not yet. I expect they will telephone when they can tell us anything concrete."

"Sorry I wasn't here when it happened," Frank said. "I — I did not get back until after the storm started and your uncle only told me this morning."

Fenn lowered her eyes to the gay yellow cloth which Daisy had used for the breakfast table that morning. It made a bright splash of colour in the usually bright room, but gloomy now with the change of weather.

"How *is* Angie?" she murmured, raising her eyes to Frank's as she spoke, seeing him redden at her mention of the other girl.

"Oh, she's fine," he murmured, beginning to rise and push his chair back against the table. "At least, she was last night. Says as soon as the weather clears you must drive over and see her."

"I'd love to. I've some shopping to

do soon. Perhaps we'll drive into town together . . . "

The telephone rang, cutting into the conversation and Frank, already on his feet, said, "I'll get it . . . "

A moment later he was back, looking at Uncle Simon and saying, "It was the hospital, Simon. It seems a couple of African children are still marooned on the island. Jason wants to mount a rescue team. He needs ropes and things. Would it be all right if I . . . ?"

Simon Chase had risen to his feet at Frank's words, as had Fenn. Simon said, "Of course you must go. There's nothing you can do around here on a morning like this."

"I'll go, too," Fenn began, beginning to hurry towards her room.

"Hold on a minute." She heard her uncle's chuckle behind her and turned to meet his twinkling eyes. Before he could say more, she said, "Don't try and tell me it's too dangerous, uncle. There must be something I can do, even if it's only to sit and keep Miss Procter company."

The twinkle in his eyes deepened. He said, "That's the spirit of your mother

269

coming out in you. I recognize the same determined chin and straight mouth. All right, child, go with Frank. Only, for heaven's sake, don't get in their way and don't offer to do anything that might prove dangerous."

At the hospital everyone was in a turmoil. Groups of women and children, chilled to the bone after their night's adventure, most of them still wearing the wet clothes they were rescued in, sat huddled together on the verandah. Even the kitchen was full of them, but Fenn noticed how the small staff of nurses, headed by Nurse Yasmin; prodded the tiny children, the picanins, closer towards the huge old fashioned stove, dispensing hot drinks as fast as they could make them.

A huge pot of stew boiled on the top of the stove and Fenn offered to watch this, thus relieving the nurses for other, more important duties. She made hot chocolate, milk and beef drinks for the next hour or so, coaxing the children to swallow. The tiny ones she helped their mother's to change, Yasmin producing a quantity of clothes from the wards. Miss

Procter came in to see how they were getting on, looking so pale and wan that Fenn's heart went out to her.

She shushed the elderly woman away, saying, "*You* should still be in bed. Jason would be so cross if he could see you now."

Miss Procter smiled. "Probably he would, but as he's not here I think I'll stay and help, and," looking pointedly at the huddle of women and children in the kitchen, some of the tiny picanins crying gustily, "I think you could do with it."

But Fenn was adamant. "No, really, dear, we're managing fine. Do go back to bed. You don't look at all well."

But Miss Procter was not to be put off. "Nonsense. I feel fine. Come on, now," making towards a tiny girl who sat at her mother's feet, mouth open in a lusty yell, "let's see what we can do for these poor mites. Jason can look them over for injuries when he returns but in the meantime we can see to their comforts." Turning to where a young African nurse hovered near the doorway, she added, "See if there are any more spare clothes in that big cupboard of mine in the hall.

271

Some woollen jerseys and things . . . "

Later, while they sipped hot tea, Miss Procter told Fenn, "Jason is leading a rescue team across the river to that island in the middle. It seems there were a couple of African children marooned there, one of them injured. Jason didn't know how bad, but if I know him he won't rest until he has got them over and at Mluba Hill." Looking at Fenn she added, softly, "There's nothing to do but wait, and hope."

A spasm of anxiety flickered across her face as she spoke. "It won't be easy, dear, the waiting. It never is."

Fenn realized without saying that the older woman knew exactly how she felt about Jason. About her love for him and the terrible anxiety she was feeling. Holding out one hand she squeezed the other woman's, and words were unnecessary between them, for didn't they both love the young doctor with a deep abiding love, even if in a different way?

It was not easy. All that long day Fenn waited for the sight of a mud-covered Land-rover, haunted by the thought of

Jason and the thin rope and the raging rushing torrent of river over which he would cross . . .

She thought of it as they crossed weeks ago, of how frightened she had been and of how much worse it would be after last night's terrible storm. In the early afternoon the phone rang and Helene's voice, sounding slightly hysterical, asked how Jason was. Miss Procter told her that so far there was no news but that it shouldn't be long now.

"With this storm it will be dark soon," Helene almost wailed. "Surely you've heard *some*thing?"

"Nothing, dear. Don't you want to come over and join the waiters? Fenn and me and the rest of our staff?"

"Don't be silly! Come out in this weather! You must be joking."

Miss Procter shrugged and replaced the receiver with the words, "All right, Helene, I'll tell him as soon as I see him."

To Fenn's anxious look she smiled, a grim little smile, and murmured, "As though the dear man will want to go tearing over to her grandfather's farm as soon as he gets out of this! He'll be tired out. I wouldn't let him go anyway, even if he wanted to."

"Talking about being tired out," Fenn smiled, "you look as though you could do with a lie down. Why don't you go to your room for a couple of hours and I'll tell you as soon as Jason and the rescue party arrive back?"

Miss Procter pushed back the mass of white hair on her temple with a weary hand. "Do you know, I think I will. I didn't realize how tired I still was. But how about you, dear? Aren't you tired yet? You've had a long day . . . "

Fenn shook her head. "No, I'm all right. I'll bring you in a fresh cup of tea as soon as you're settled."

How could she say that she *had* to be here when Jason returned? *Had* to see his face again, know that he was all right. Later as she sat talking to Miss Procter at her bedside, tray of tea beside them on a small table, she said thoughtfully, thinking of Helene's conversation on the telephone, "She's so in love with Jason that she must be worried sick."

"Helene in love!" Miss Procter looked

at her over the rim of her cup. "Are you sure we're talking about the same woman?"

At Fenn's look of enquiry, she added, smiling, "The only person Helene is in love with is herself. A more selfish girl I've yet to meet. Although her grandfather adores her I have no doubt he'll be relieved when she returns to the city."

"I . . . " Fenn swallowed. "She's leaving here? Is — is Jason going too?"

"Of course not." Miss Procter's voice was filled with scorn. "I gather there's a new attraction in the city, some fashionable painter who wants to do her portrait."

"But — but I thought she and Jason . . . "

"I think she thought so, too, but it hasn't worked out like that, Fenn." She looked at the young girl, smiling. "Jason and I talked last night for a long time, after you had gone. We learned a lot of things about each other we've never learned before, in spite of my years of working with him. Jason is" — she paused, frowning. "a strange man, Fenn. Not easily understandable. You think you know him, then he'll do or say something so completely contradictory that you realize you never really knew him at all."

Fenn grinned wryly. "I'm beginning to realize that, too."

She stood up, seeing Miss Procter's eyes beginning to close and took the empty cup from her. She picked up the tray of tea things and said, "Try and get some sleep, dear. I'll let you know as soon as we hear any news."

Outside the rain was over, a watery sun trying hard to pierce the grey clouds. But the air was much warmer, promising a hot day tomorrow. The children and their mothers in the hospital kitchen seemed more settled. Many had fallen asleep on blankets which the nurses had provided. A few, a very few, still whined a little and their mothers hugged and comforted them as best they could. Nurse Yasmin, seeing Fenn's face, pale and weary with the strain which she was under, said, "Go outside and get some fresh air, Miss Fenn. It will do you good. The doctor should not be long now. We had a message that they had rescued the two children and were back on this side of the river. He should be back any moment . . . "

"Could you let Miss Procter know?" Fenn murmured. "I promised to tell her as soon as we knew."

"If she's asleep I won't wake her," the little nurse promised. "But I will tell her, don't worry."

Pulling on a raincoat, for the air was still damp in spite of the sun's watery attempts to dry the soaked countryside, Fenn walked down the flight of steps to the garden and made her way across the muddy garden. So absorbed was she in her own thoughts that she did not see the tall figure emerge from the trees by the car park, and she ran full tilt into him.

She gasped as hard arms closed around her. Her head went back and she blinked as she gazed up at Jason's face, so dangerously close to hers.

"Hold still, I was coming to you," he said, smiling that wry smile that did such things to her heart.

"You got back?" she gasped, feeling foolish, feeling, oh she did not know what she felt with his arms about her like that.

"Yes, I got back." Still holding her he gazed round at the deserted garden, the trees under which they stood still dripping, the ground almost liquid mud at the ferocity of the downpour. "Why are you wandering around the garden like this? Surely you should be inside with the others?"

"I've — I've been there all day. I was worried about you."

He stared down at her, at the dark hair spangled with raindrops. Like diamonds, he caught himself thinking. He put up one hand to touch it, curling one long strand about his finger. "Why should you worry about me?" he demanded.

"We're getting damp," she murmured, tying to pull away from his arms, scared, confused, excited at the thought that Helene was no longer a threat to her happiness. "Please, Jason . . . "

As she spoke his name he said something that was half strangled in his throat, then he swung her almost off her feet as another gust of rain fell from the heavens, soaking them in moments. The tiny schoolroom where aeons ago she had visited with Miss Procter was a matter of a hundred yards away and he pulled her towards there, muttering below his breath, "This blasted rain . . . "

He pushed her inside and she staggered, rain-wet, yet laughing, happy that she was again with him, no matter what the circumstances.

He closed the door and they faced each other in the murky light. He looked rather grim, and weary, his black hair plastered to his forehead above eyes that longed for sleep. "Why should you worry about me?" he once more demanded.

"Y — You know why, — that river, I realized how dangerous it would be . . . Anyway," glaring at him defiantly, "Why shouldn't I worry about you if I feel like it?" She drew a step away from him, from his tall, dark maleness; the look in his eyes that she hardly dared meet with her own.

His mouth twisted wryly. "A good question. I cannot deny it's a free world and one can worry about anyone one wants to, but I would still like to know why." He advanced on her and suddenly the world was silent all around them. The rain had stopped as suddenly as it had started and in the silence Fenn heard the pounding of her heart.

"You're — you're tired, Jason," she began, turning away. "Come on, let's go back to the hospital. Miss Procter . . ."

"Damn Miss Procter!" Mouth agape, she stared at him. "Really, Jason . . ."

"Miss Procter is a woman who is quite capable of looking after herself," he told her. "Meanwhile, you and I have a life to live and I intend to do something about it, right now." He was close now and she could see every detail of his face, lean, proud, but infinitely weary after his dangerous exploits of the morning. Her very breath seemed to die in her throat as his hands clasped hers, holding lightly but with intention.

"Can't we talk about that life, Fenn, without you wanting to get back to Miss Procter or your uncle?"

"Why, I — I suppose so," she murmured, dropping her eyes to her hands clasped so tightly in his. "If you insist."

"I *do* insist." His smile was fleeting and the tenderness was plain to see in his eyes as he gazed down on her dark head, still damp from the rain.

"Let me tell you something," he went on. "Helene came to see me a few days ago. She told me I had the choice of following her to the clinic in Cape Town that her grandfather had organized for me, or she would go off with this artist chap she met there last year. I had a choice, she said. It so happens that an ultimatum of this kind did little for my feelings for her. I'm afraid I told her so, in no uncertain way."

"She — she telephoned the hospital a little while ago," Fenn murmured. "She wanted to see you." She raised her eyes to meet his. "Why, the other night, in the car, did you say your path must run in different ways to mine? Why — why cannot they run together?" Realizing the incredible words she had spoken, Fenn raised her hands to her face, covering the blush that swept up to her hair line. But suddenly his own hands were cupping her face, forcing her own, oh, so gently, away. "Fenn, my dearest!" she felt herself go tense at his touch and then his lips were on hers without mercy.

"Don't let's waste our time talking

about Helene," he murmured. "There are so many more important things to discuss." He kissed her hair. "From the moment I saw you in the hospital grounds, looking so fierce and protective towards your little African mother, I loved you. But it was something I could not speak about. My life was here. You were here for such a short time. I didn't even know if you could love a man who wanted to live this kind of life above all others. Then I found you had a courage that very few girls these days possess. I could only hope that you liked it here in the valley so much that you wouldn't want to go back to England."

She drew back a little and smiled, teasingly. "Easier said than done. I don't even know if my uncle wants me to stay much longer . . . "

"Who said anything about living with your uncle." He quirked a black eyebrow. "Do you think you could manage to put up with me, here at Mluba Hill, permanently?"

Fenn nodded happily. Yes, she would live at Mluba Hill with Jason and the people she loved. Even now she was planning a wedding, a wedding that would coincide with the next jacaranda season, for wasn't that the prettiest time of all, here in the valley, with the sky a deep, pure blue and the blossoms beneath them matching in colour?

"Yes," she breathed, feeling his arms fold about her close, oh, so closely and comfortingly. "Here I will live with you for ever, my Jason."

THE END

NURSE ALICE IN LOVE
Theresa Charles

Accepting the post of nurse to little Fernie Sherrod, Alice Everton could not guess at the romance, suspense and danger which lay ahead at the Sherrod's isolated estate.

POIROT INVESTIGATES
Agatha Christie

Two things bind these eleven stories together — the brilliance and uncanny skill of the diminutive Belgian detective, and the stupidity of his Watson-like partner, Captain Hastings.

LET LOOSE THE TIGERS
Josephine Cox

Queenie promised to find the long-lost son of the frail, elderly murderess, Hannah Jason. But her enquiries threatened to unlock the cage where crucial secrets had long been held captive.

TIGER TIGER
Frank Ryan

A young man involved in drugs is found murdered. This is the first event which will draw Detective Inspector Sandy Woodings into a whirlpool of murder and deceit.

CAROLINE MINUSCULE
Andrew Taylor

Caroline Minuscule, a medieval script, is the first clue to the whereabouts of a cache of diamonds. The search becomes a deadly kind of fairy story in which several murders have an other-worldly quality.

LONG CHAIN OF DEATH
Sarah Wolf

During the Second World War four American teenagers from the same town join the Army together. Forty-two years later, the son of one of the soldiers realises that someone is systematically wiping out the families of the four men.

THE LISTERDALE MYSTERY
Agatha Christie

Twelve short stories ranging from the light-hearted to the macabre, diverse mysteries ingeniously and plausibly contrived and convincingly unravelled.

TO BE LOVED
Lynne Collins

Andrew married the woman he had always loved despite the knowledge that Sarah married him for reasons of her own. So much heartache could have been avoided if only he had known how vital it was to be loved.

ACCUSED NURSE
Jane Converse

Paula found herself accused of a crime which could cost her her job, her nurse's reputation, and even the man she loved, unless the truth came to light.

THE PLEASURES OF AGE
Robert Morley

The author, British stage and screen star, now eighty, is enjoying the pleasures of age. He has drawn on his experiences to write this witty, entertaining and informative book.

THE VINEGAR SEED
Maureen Peters

The first book in a trilogy which follows the exploits of two sisters who leave Ireland in 1861 to seek their fortune in England.

A VERY PAROCHIAL MURDER
John Wainwright

A mugging in the genteel seaside town turned to murder when the victim died. Then the body of a young tearaway is washed ashore and Detective Inspector Lyle is determined that a second killing will not go unpunished.

DEATH ON A
HOT SUMMER NIGHT
Anne Infante

Micky Douglas is either accident-prone or someone is trying to kill him. He finds himself caught in a desperate race to save his ex-wife and others from a ruthless gang.

HOLD DOWN A SHADOW
Geoffrey Jenkins

Maluti Rider, with the help of four of the world's most wanted men, is determined to destroy the Katse Dam and release a killer flood.

THAT NICE MISS SMITH
Nigel Morland

A reconstruction and reassessment of the trial in 1857 of Madeleine Smith, who was acquitted by a verdict of Not Proven of poisoning her lover, Emile L'Angelier.

SEASONS OF MY LIFE
Hannah Hauxwell
and Barry Cockcroft

The story of Hannah Hauxwell's struggle to survive on a desolate farm in the Yorkshire Dales with little money, no electricity and no running water.

TAKING OVER
Shirley Lowe and Angela Ince

A witty insight into what happens when women take over in the boardroom and their husbands take over chores, children and chickenpox.

AFTER MIDNIGHT STORIES,
The Fourth Book Of

A collection of sixteen of the best of today's ghost stories, all different in style and approach but all combining to give the reader that special midnight shiver.

DEATH TRAIN
Robert Byrne

The tale of a freight train out of control and leaking a paralytic nerve gas that turns America's West into a scene of chemical catastrophe in which whole towns are rendered helpless.

THE ADVENTURE
OF THE
CHRISTMAS PUDDING
Agatha Christie

In the introduction to this short story collection the author wrote "This book of Christmas fare may be described as 'The Chef's Selection'. I am the Chef!"

RETURN TO BALANDRA
Grace Driver

Returning to her Caribbean island home, Suzanne looks forward to being with her parents again, but most of all she longs to see Wim van Branden, a coffee planter she has known all her life.

SKINWALKERS
Tony Hillerman

The peace of the land between the sacred mountains is shattered by three murders. Is a 'skinwalker', one who has rejected the harmony of the Navajo way, the murderer?

A PARTICULAR PLACE
Mary Hocking

How is Michael Hoath, newly arrived vicar of St. Hilary's, to meet the demands of his flock and his strained marriage? Further complications follow when he falls hopelessly in love with a married parishioner.

A MATTER OF MISCHIEF
Evelyn Hood

A saga of the weaving folk in 18th century Scotland. Physician Gavin Knox was desperately seeking a cure for the pox that ravaged the slums of Glasgow and Paisley, but his adored wife, Margaret, stood in the way.

DEAD SPIT
Janet Edmonds

Government vet Linus Rintoul attempts to solve a mystery which plunges him into the esoteric world of pedigree dogs, murder and terrorism, and Crufts Dog Show proves to be far more exciting than he had bargained for . . .

A BARROW IN THE BROADWAY
Pamela Evans

Adopted by the Gordillo family, Rosie Goodson watched their business grow from a street barrow to a chain of supermarkets. But passion, bitterness and her unhappy marriage aliented her from them.

THE GOLD AND THE DROSS
Eleanor Farnes

Lorna found it hard to make ends meet for herself and her mother and then by chance she met two men — one a famous author and one a rich banker. But could she really expect to be happy with either man?

THE SONG OF THE PINES
Christina Green

Taken to a Greek island as substitute for David Nicholas's secretary, Annie quickly falls prey to the island's charms and to the charms of both Marcus, the Greek, and David himself.

GOODBYE DOCTOR GARLAND
Marjorie Harte

The story of a woman doctor who gave too much to her profession and almost lost her personal happiness.

DIGBY
Pamela Hill

Welcomed at courts throughout Europe, Kenelm Digby was the particular favourite of the Queen of France, who wanted him to be her lover, but the beautiful Venetia was the mainspring of his life.

PREJUDICED WITNESS
Dilys Gater

Fleur Rowley finds when she leaves London for her 'author's retreat' in the wilds of North Wales that she is drawn, in spite of herself, into an old tragedy.

GENTLE TYRANT
Lucy Gillen

Working as Ross McAdam's secretary, Laura couldn't imagine why his bitchy ex-wife should see her as a rival.

DEAR CAPRICE
Juliet Gray

Clifford Fortune married Caprice but his brother, Luke, knew the marriage was a mistake. He could allow himself to love Caprice blindly but that would be betraying his own brother.

IN PALE BATTALIONS
Robert Goddard

Leonora Galloway has waited all her life to learn the truth about her father, slain on the Somme before she was born, the truth about the death of her mother and the mystery of an unsolved wartime murder.

A DREAM FOR TOMORROW
Grace Goodwin

In her new position as resident nurse at Coombe Magna, Karen Stevens has to bear the emnity of the beautiful Lisa, secretary to the doctor-on-call.

AFTER EMMA
Sheila Hocken

Following the author's previous auto-biographies — EMMA & I, and EMMA & Co., she relates more of the hilarious (and sometimes despairing) antics of her guide dogs.

LEAVE IT TO THE HANGMAN
Bill Knox

Dope, dynamite, guns, currency — whatever it was John Kilburn and his son Pat had known how to get it in or out of England, if the price was right. But their luck changed when one of them killed a cop.

A VIOLENT END
Emma Page

To Chief Inspector Kelsey there was no shortage of suspects when Karen Boland was murdered, and that was before he discovered that she stood to inherit substantially at twenty-one.

SILENCE IN HANOVER CLOSE
Anne Perry

In 1884 Robert York is found brutally murdered at his home in Hanover Close. When, three years later, Inspector Pitt is asked to investigate, the murder remains unsolved.

A RARE BENEDICTINE
Ellis Peters

Three vintage tales of medieval intrigue and treachery featuring the author's monastic sleuth Brother Cadfael.

POIROT'S EARLY CASES
Agatha Christie

In this collection of eighteen stories, Hercule Poirot begins his celebrated career in crime.

THE SILVER LINK
— THE SILKEN LIE
Lynn Granger

Elspeth is determined to preserve her Scottish heritage and the Elliot name, but running Everanlea, a large hill farm, presents problems.